PROM KING

THE FINCREDIBLE DIARY OF FIN SPENCER

Ciaran Murtagh is a writer of books and television programmes

for children. Ciaran lives in London — to find out more about what

he's writing and appearing in, follow him on Twitter @ciaranmurtagh

or head over to

www.ciaranmurtagh.com

Books by Ciaran Murtagh

CHARLIE FLINT AND THE DINOS
Dinopants
Dinopoo
Dinoburps
Dinoball

BALTHAZAR THE GENIE
Genie in Training
Genie in Trouble
Genie in a Trap

THE FINCREDIBLE DIARY OF FIN SPENCER
Stuntboy
Megastar
Action Hero
Prom King

PROM KING
THE
FINCREDIBLE DIARY
OF
FIN SPENCER

by CIARAN MURTAGH

with illustrations throughout by TIM WESSON

Piccadilly
PRESS

First published in Great Britain in 2016
by Piccadilly Press
80–81 Wimpole Street, London, W1G 9RE
www.piccadillypress.co.uk

A CIP catalogue record for this book is available from the British Library.

ISBN: 978-1-848-12558-2
also available as an ebook

1 3 5 7 9 10 8 6 4 2

Printed and bound by Clays Ltd, St Ives PLC

Piccadilly Press is an imprint of Bonnier Zaffre,
a Bonnier Publishing Company
www.bonnierpublishing.com

For Bonnie,
who arrived too late
to appear in the book,
apart from here . . .

MONDAY

My name's Fin Spencer and my life is falling apart like a pair of pound-shop pants. If I don't act fast I'll be **Fin Spencer, Right Royal Loser!** And that can't happen. I'm a **Stuntboy Megastar Action Hero** in training — I've got standards to maintain!

Things are so bad that, as you can see, I've decided to break out the **magic diary** again. Now, I know what you're thinking.

You're thinking there's no such thing as a magic diary and anyone who thinks differently is as silly as a sausage in a swimming pool. But trust me, *this* diary is magic, and I'll prove it.

There's just one problem. This diary is also <u>trouble</u>. It's got me out of loads of scrapes, but it's got me into just as many! But I've got it mastered now. Trust me! Nothing can go wrong. I'll use it one last time and then I'll put it away forever. Promise. I mean, I know I've said that LOADS of times before, but this time it's a <u>REAL</u> promise, not one of those fake promises you make but don't really mean, like:

Of course I won't eat the chocolate cake

Or

Or

That last one nearly worked, until I asked for free popcorn and a back massage too!

Anyway, that's not the point. The point is in two weeks there's going to be a school prom and obviously, as the coolest kid in our school (if not the ENTIRE UNIVERSE), I should be Prom King. Sure, until this morning I didn't even know what a prom was, let alone that I should be king of it. But I was born to rule. I'd be a natural. I could get used to having servants, I've got the perfect head for a crown and I'm pretty good at waving. What more does one need? See? I've even got the lingo! There's just one problem. Mrs Johnson, my teacher, has ended my reign before I even got a chance to sit on the throne! So now I need help.

I need the diary.

I should have known today was going to be a

as soon as I woke up. Mum's pregnant, which means I have to do 'A little more around the house'. Which we all know is mum-speak for 'Wait on her hand and foot.' So this morning I had to help her into her shoes, lay the table and bring her a cup of tea before I even had a shower. But if you thought that would be the end of my jobs, you'd be wrong!

After I've helped Mum I have to make my own breakfast. Yes! You heard right! I have to go to the cupboard, get out the COCO SNAPS, go to <u>another</u> cupboard, get out a bowl, go to the drawer and get out a spoon

. . . and don't even get me started

on the milk! There's

three different sorts in

the fridge and one of

them is made from

soya, which isn't

even a cow. Unless

the cow's name is

Soya, but whoever heard of a cow

called Soya?

By the time I get to school I'm already

feeling more stressed than a cat at a dog

show . . . Luckily, my best friend **JOSH**

DOYLE and the new kid **BLAKE ROMNEY**

were waiting for me at the gates. **BLAKE**

is from America and he's come to our school

SOYA

How rude!

on an exchange visit. Every word out of his mouth sounds really cool, even if I'm not always sure what he's going on about.

Last week we were in the playground when he leaned over and said

Sweet pants, Fin.

I couldn't believe my ears! How did **BLAKE ROMNEY** know I was wearing my emergency 'Farter Christmas' pants?? Did he have X-ray Pant Vision or something? I spent the next half hour hiding in the toilet looking for a hole in my trousers. Then **JOSH** came and explained that 'pants' was American for 'trousers'. So **BLAKE** wasn't actually saying nice pants, he was saying <u>nice trousers</u>, which is still a bit weird if you ask me.

Then, last weekend **BLAKE** asked me and **JOSH** to 'go and hang at the mall', which sounded like something cool from the movies, but it turns out it just meant 'go and sit in the shopping centre'. Which is about as exciting as watching a snail marathon. We still had a good time, though, because **BLAKE** told us all about the new TV shows that are coming our way this 'fall' — that's American for autumn, apparently — and then he treated us to burgers. Result!

In registration Mrs Johnson reminded us that it was only two weeks until the summer holidays and everyone cheered — even Mrs Johnson, which is just rude if you ask me. Once the cheering died down **BLAKE** asked what the theme of the prom was going to be and everyone got confused. **What was a prom?**

It turns out 'Prom' was Blake-speak for 'End of year disco'. But the way **BLAKE** described it made it sound amazing. There would be dancing, food, limousines — the works. It all sounded really glamorous. But I could tell Mrs Johnson was about to say no, until **BLAKE** said something that made her think again.

And best of all, it's organised by the students.

Mrs Johnson's eyes lit up like a radioactive lighthouse. She realised that if we swapped the end of year disco for a school prom she wouldn't have to lift a finger to organise it!

Suddenly it sounded like 'An opportunity for cross cultural awareness.' Which we all know is teacher-speak for 'One less job for me to do!' She set us a whole page of maths equations and raced off to clear the idea with Mr Finch, the headmaster.

By the time Mrs Johnson got back I'd done more equations than a NASA scientist. She and Mr Finch had decided the prom was going to be for our whole year group, not just my class. This was going to be one mega party! The students would form a Prom Committee to organise it, made up of volunteers from the three classes in our year. Huh! Who'd volunteer for that?

Organising your own end of year party sounded about as much fun as a day at a pensioners' theme park.

FIN SPENCER'S RIGHT ROYAL RULE 1
IF YOU HAVE TO ORGANISE YOUR OWN PARTY, IT'S NO LONGER A PARTY. IT'S <u>WORK</u>!

BLAKE put his hand up to volunteer anyway. Which kind of made sense, I guess — he was the one who'd come up with the idea in the first place, so it was only right that he should do all the hard work. Then the usual suspects put their hands up too, including **CLAUDIA RONSON**, her best friend **LUCY** and **BRAD RADLEY**, the meanest kid in school. Why did **BRAD RADLEY** want to be on the Prom Committee? Maybe he'd misheard the question and thought he was on a bomb committee or something . . .

With the Prom Committee chosen, **BLAKE** told us more about the prom tradition. Apparently we have to have a Prom King and Prom Queen, voted for by the students in our year. Now that sounded right up my street — or should that be *castle*?

And if **CLAUDIA RONSON** could be Prom Queen then it would be <u>even better!</u>

CLAUDIA and I are kind of boyfriend and girlfriend but it hasn't been going too well recently. It might have something to do with the date we went on a couple of weeks ago to the crazy golf course. It had all been going fine until about halfway through when I hit my ball at the miniature windmill. I was trying to get it through the little hole but instead the ball pinged off the windmill's sail and headed straight for my face.

Luckily, I ducked.

Unluckily, **CLAUDIA** didn't.

I ended up winning and she ended up with a headache. I decided to give her some time to cool down but that was two weeks ago and we haven't spoken properly since. Being Prom King and Prom Queen would be the most amazing way to patch things up between us.

No such luck! Mrs Johnson had decided that in order to be considered for Prom King or Queen you had to be on the Prom Committee. That was so unfair! If she'd said that before asking for volunteers then I'd definitely have put my hand up.

Mrs Johnson said that was the point! She said that the sort of person who would make a good Prom King was

20

The sort of person who volunteered to do something nice for others without thinking of themselves.

It was a  **DISASTER!**

My first prom was ruined before it had even started! I HAD to get on that Prom Committee. It was the only way I could be considered for Prom King, and if I wasn't king, **CLAUDIA** couldn't be my queen.

I ran home after school to get this diary to fix it.

Before I could get upstairs, though, Mum wanted me to help unload the shopping from the car and unpack it in the kitchen. That would have been bad enough but while I was figuring out whether you put ketchup in the fridge or on a shelf my little sister ELLIE started practising her violin. She wants to join the school orchestra but every time she plays it sounds like Dracula running his fingernails down a blackboard. It helped me decide where to put some of the toilet rolls though. I opened them on the spot and shoved loo paper in my ears!

By the time I'd finished it was dinnertime and Mum and Dad started to discuss baby names. Apparently I had to take the loo paper out and join in! On Thursday night it's the scan to find out if it's **a boy or a girl**, and Mum wants to have some names in mind so we can decide before the baby arrives. But Mum and Dad have some really **weird ideas**. Currently they want to call the baby Monty, after a great-uncle who died 1,000 years ago or something. **P<u>oor kid!</u>** I think it makes him sound like **a spaniel**.

I ran upstairs to get **the diary** before things could get any worse.

We all remember the diary rules, right?

FIN SPENCER'S
FINCREDIBLE
DIARY RULES

1. The diary only changes the things I say and do or wished I'd said and done

2. It only changes things if I write about what I wish I'd done **ON THE DAY** they happen

3. Diaries are still for `losers`. It's only this one that's cool.

So here goes. Today I put my hand up and volunteered to be on the Prom Committee. **Got that, diary?** A right royal date with **CLAUDIA** and my reputation as <u>coolest kid in class</u> are depending on you!

TUESDAY

When I got up this morning Mum was already downstairs. Apparently she'd been up for ages with her back. Which just got me confused. How could she have been up without it? On the plus side she'd poured me a bowl of COCO SNAPS. On the minus side it wasn't quite as big as I'd been getting used to. At least getting your own cereal in the morning meant you could decide how much you had . . .

When I got to school, **BLAKE ROMNEY** was waiting for me. He wanted to remind me that the first Prom Committee meeting was this lunchtime and apparently there was lots to do. I grinned from ear to ear. That meant I was on the committee – result! Well done, diary! My quest to be Prom King was back on track.

In class, Mrs Johnson announced that **BLAKE** had volunteered to be Committee Chair. I asked if that meant we all got to sit on him, but no one laughed. Apparently it just means he's in charge, which is fine by me, I don't want to do too much work!

After registration we had history. I'd been so caught up in this whole prom thing last night that I'd forgotten we were supposed to be researching our family tree for homework. I didn't see the point. Who'd be interested in my family tree? My family are so boring they'd make trainspotters look like bungee-jumpers. Mr Moore told us that we had a few minutes to finish our homework while he did some marking, so I got to work.

I decided to make my family tree a bit more interesting and by the time I'd finished my dad was Henry VIII and my mum was Lady Gaga. Then Mr Moore made us stand in front of the class and read them out. Oops.w

By the time I got to Mr Bean, my granddad, Mr Moore had had enough. He gave me a detention and told me I needed to 'Grow up' which we all know is teacher-speak for 'Be more boring!' But even detention couldn't spoil my mood.

At break **JOSH**, **BLAKE** and I played football — or soccer, as **BLAKE** insists on calling it. **CLAUDIA**'s watching and I'm about to score a killer goal when **SAM LUTHER** walks across the pitch and ruins my shot. Just as I'm just getting over the disappointment he has the cheek to ask to play! **SAM** isn't in our class and to be honest I don't know him that well so I let him play for the other team. I'm not being nice. They're rubbish. Prepare to be thrashed!

Turns out it was ME who was getting the thrashing. **SAM** is a demon football player! Before I know it he's got the ball, chipped it over his head <u>and</u> scored a goal! To make it worse, **CLAUDIA** gives him a massive round of applause. Typical! I spend the rest of break time losing at football to **SAM LUTHER** while **CLAUDIA** claps his every move.

After lunch we head to a spare classroom to have our first Prom Committee meeting. It turns out there's loads of stuff that needs to be organised before the prom and **BLAKE**'s got a list that's longer than a giant's loo roll.

PROPERTY OF FEE FI FO FUM

1

We need a venue, a photographer, some tickets, a theme, decorations, a band . . .

For a moment I stop listening. Did **BLAKE** just say we needed a band? Well that's an easy one to solve! There's only ONE band in this school worth listening to and that's MY band, System of the Future! We should definitely play. I can see it all: I'll storm the gig, be made Prom King and end up doing the final dance with **CLAUDIA**! It couldn't be better. There's just one problem. The band has got three members . . . and one of them is in America!

When **BLAKE** came over here, the school sent **CLIFF SHRAPNEL**, our guitar player, over there.

I quickly brainstorm ways to solve this:

1 Have the prom in America — <u>too hard!</u>

2 Fly **CLIFF** back — <u>too expensive!</u>

3 Run a really long guitar lead under the sea — <u>too complicated!</u>

4 Let him play by video call — <u>too technical!</u>

5 Fire **CLIFF** and find a replacement — <u>the obvious choice!</u>

I must have been daydreaming for a bit longer than I thought because when I come round things seem to have been sorted out. The prom is happening in the school hall and tickets go on sale tomorrow. **BRAD RADLEY**'s dad runs a print shop so he's in charge of printing them up, they'll be on a first-come first-served basis so we have to be quick.

I double-check what's been decided about the band. Apparently there's going to be open auditions on Friday. **No worries!** That gives me three days to find a new guitarist, storm the audition and **top the bill** at the prom. **Easy.** I also decide to check whether I've been made Prom King yet. **BLAKE** smiles and says it doesn't work like that. You have to be nominated by two of your classmates. Everyone who is nominated gets put on the voting paper on prom night. Then everyone votes, the winners are announced and the Prom King and Queen are crowned.

Is that all? This is going to be easy!

After school I decide to ask **CLAUDIA** to be my prom date and head off to find her. Unfortunately Mr Finch finds me first —

had I forgotten about detention? It turns out I had! I spend the next forty-five minutes trying to research my real family tree while Mr Finch 'does some marking'. Which we all know is headmaster-speak for 'play games on the computer'.

Once I'm out of detention I head to **CLAUDIA**'s house. When I get there I see **SAM LUTHER** leaving. That's weird! I knock on the door and **CLAUDIA** answers. I apologise about the whole windmill lumpy-head thing and ask her to be my prom date. She says she's sorry, but she's already said yes to **SAM**.

SAM LUTHER, is she joking?

Apparently it's not a girlfriend/boyfriend thing, he's just really nice and she thought it would be good to go with him.

That's not the point! She's <u>MY</u> girlfriend!

CLAUDIA gets a bit upset and says she's not my girlfriend, she hasn't even spoken to me since the whole crazy golf thing and perhaps if I'd actually apologised earlier or asked her first she might have said yes. Too late now, though, isn't it?

This is a **DISASTER!**

I don't have a prom date and it's all because of that detention. If I'd got up early and done my history homework like I was supposed to then none of this would have happened — instead I would have come straight to **CLAUDIA**'s and put things right.

<u>I need my diary</u> so I rush straight home to get it. Before I can get upstairs, Dad stops me. He's bought himself a new camera so he can 'Capture the birth on film'. Which is dad-speak for 'Gross out relatives forever'! He wants to practise using it and needs a model. Well, if he needs a model he came to the right place! I make **Brad Pitt look like Quasimodo** on a daily basis!

Unfortunately Dad doesn't know how to use his own camera and after forty-five minutes he's taken 167 photos of my nostrils.

Brilliant! He goes back upstairs to read the manual again.

For dinner Mum has made us something she calls a **Broccolicious Broccoli bake.** It's the third one this month and it makes the whole house stink like **a hamster's armpit.** She keeps making disgusting **broccoli-based food** because the baby's giving her these weird cravings.

1 **Broc Choc Chip Ice Cream –** with broccoli flake!

2 **Broccoli Hot Dog –** without the sausage, or the bun!

3 **Stuffed Broccoli Surprise –** stuffed with more broccoli . . . surprise!

Gross! Gross! Gross!

I don't know why she wants a baby anyway.

I mean, Mum's already had the perfect child – **me!** She shouldn't push her luck. Look at how my little sister **ELLIE** turned out. **We don't want another one of those.**

After dinner I decide to cheer myself up with a bit of TV when Mum and Dad hijack the sofa. They've become addicted to this terrible Swedish detective programme called Das Kop Shau. It's in black and white, nobody dies and everyone just stares at the sea. Honestly, who wants to watch a TV programme where you have to read subtitles? **Then Mum has an idea.** She thinks they should name the baby Klaus after the handsome detective in the show. I laugh and say, 'What, like Santa Klaus?' Nobody else finds it funny. I decide to head upstairs and knock up some posters for guitarist auditions.

With posters printed and all my **chores** done I'm about to settle down for a quick game of **DEATH SQUADRON** when **ELLIE** cranks up her violin. It sounds like she's killing a chicken. It's impossible to concentrate on the game so I shove some more toilet roll in my ears and break out the diary.

I need to sort out a prom date. There's no way **CLAUDIA** should be going with **SAM LUTHER**. It's obvious we're meant to be together. If I hadn't got a detention then I could have asked her out before **SAM** did and we'd still be on target for becoming prom royalty.

So diary, THIS MORNING I GOT UP EARLY AND DID MY HISTORY HOMEWORK, PROPERLY! You can still leave my granddad as Mr Bean if you want though. It kind of suits him and no one will notice!

WEDNESDAY

This morning I'm woken really early by the sound of a cat being murdered. Or so I thought. It turns out it's **ELLIE** practising her violin for an orchestra audition she's got this afternoon. Unless the orchestra has a new piece of music to play called 'Dead Cat Symphony', there's no way she's getting in.

Before I head for school I empty my piggy bank. I've been saving up for the new **DEATH SQUADRON** game — **DEATH SQUADRON: ANNIHILATION** — for ages. It's only out in America at the moment but it'll be on sale here soon and I've been planning on spending my summer holidays blasting **JOSH** up and down the computer screen. But the prom is way more important than that. I need to get a ticket and I've got just enough saved up.

I stuff the band audition posters in my bag and head for school. In registration the prom is all anyone is talking about. **BRAD RADLEY** is boasting that his dad is going to hire him a stretch limousine to take him to the prom! Some kids get all the luck — my dad wouldn't even hire me a donkey.

It looks like I might need a bit more cash in order to do this prom **FIN-STYLE**, but my piggy bank's emptier than a supermodel's fridge. I'll need to think of something.

After registration Mrs Johnson hands back the history homework I apparently did yesterday morning — thanks, diary! Mr Moore has complimented me on my 'completely unremarkable family' and given me a B. 'Unremarkable'? I can't help that! I tried to spice it up by saying my mum was Lady Gaga and he got angry, now he's not happy with the truth. This homework is impossible!

FIN SPENCER'S RIGHT ROYAL RULE 2

TEACHERS ARE NEVER HAPPY. IT'S BEST TO ACCEPT THAT AND NOT EVEN TRY!

I'm about to get angry when I realise this means the diary worked and the date with **CLAUDIA** should be back on — result!

BRAD RADLEY and **BLAKE ROMNEY** have set up a stall in the sports hall to sell prom tickets at break time. **BRAD**'s dad has printed them and they look great. In order to be first in the queue, I pretend to have a toilet emergency just before the bell rings, and head for the sports hall. I am a genius. As soon as the bell goes there's a long line down the corridor with Fin Spencer, future Prom King, right at the front — double result!

CLAUDIA comes to find me. She tells me she's really looking forward to the date — way to go, diary! — and thanks me for buying her ticket. Er, what is she talking about? Before I have time to ask, CLAUDIA's best friend LUCY whisks her off to the loo for a chat. After she's gone, BLAKE reminds me that it's traditional for boys to buy a ticket for their prom date, which is apparently what I offered to do yesterday after taking his advice! Who made that rule up? I bet it wasn't a boy!

DISASTER!

I only have enough money for <u>one ticket,</u> so I do the decent thing and buy the ticket for **CLAUDIA**. As I hand it over she smiles and promises that this is going to be the best prom ever. I'm sure it will be, if I actually get there! This prom is turning out to be more expensive than a billionaire's birthday cake! I'll need to speak to Mum and Dad about it this evening.

Without money for a second ticket, I spend the rest of break putting up posters for the System of the Future auditions. As I'm pinning up the final one CLAUDIA sees me and says she might come along later. I tell her that's brilliant, we need someone to take notes on the different guitarists, and she heads off in a huff. What's got into her? At least she's got a prom ticket! I'll never understand girls.

After break Mr Lilley, the science teacher, asks if I'm feeling OK. I'm confused, but then he points out that I went to the loo and never came back. Apparently he was worried I might have fallen in. Everyone laughs. I try to make up an excuse but he sees right through it. It looks like I'm going to spend the rest of the lesson cleaning test tubes.

There's another committee meeting at lunchtime and **BLAKE** runs through a few more of the things we need to decide. There's going to be a dress code and all the boys need to come in a tuxedo. Great, more money I need to find! He also reminds us about the audition for Prom Band on Friday. Don't worry, **BLAKE**! It's all in hand.

Just before the meeting ends, **BLAKE** congratulates us on a successful ticket sale this morning, The prom is now officially sold out! I'm about to join in with the applause when I realise what's been said. The prom is **SOLD OUT**. But I don't have a ticket!

Well, I do but I gave it to **CLAUDIA**!

DOUBLE DISASTER!

If I don't go to the prom how can I be elected Prom King? I corner **BLAKE** after the meeting. Surely there has to be a way to get another ticket. I'll do anything to get one . . .

1 Clean the school loos with a toothbrush

2 Juggle knives on a volcano

3 Kiss Mrs Johnson — only on the cheek, though. I'm not **THAT** desperate!

BLAKE shakes his head and says he's sorry, but there's nothing he can do.

It's not fair! My date is going to the prom and I'm not. **JOSH** tries to sympathise and offers to take **CLAUDIA** instead of me. Not helping, **JOSH**! But it's OK. I'll just need to make sure the diary helped me find enough money for two tickets this morning.

Before that, though, there's the little matter of the System of the Future auditions. When I get to the school hall there's a line of people holding guitar cases waiting to audition. I immediately cheer up — people actually want to be in MY band! **CLAUDIA** is there too, I wasn't sure she'd turn up. She's got a sheaf of papers in her hand — perfect for taking notes! Nice one, **CLAUDIA**! I give her a pen and tell her to record scores out of ten, and she gets in a huff again. **I don't understand!** Why did she turn up to help if she doesn't want to be involved?

JOSH and I sit behind a table to judge the auditions. First up is a kid called **JAMES** who's in the year below. I didn't even know he knew how to play guitar!

It turns out he doesn't, he plays *air* guitar and wanted to see if it still counted. He thrashes about like a monkey in a mosh pit until **JOSH** and I make him stop. Zero points. **NEXT!**

It's a girl called **SARAH**. She actually can play guitar, the problem is she only knows how to play nursery rhymes. **System of the Future** are <u>NOT</u> playing

'Three Blind Mice' and 'The Hokey Cokey' at the school prom! Two points! NEXT!

Then **SAM LUTHER** arrives and I put my head in my hands. This kid is haunting my every move. Maybe he's a stalker? He starts to play and he knows a couple of our songs. **JOSH** likes him and thinks he should be in the band. **CLAUDIA** gives him ten points without even asking! No way! I make **CLAUDIA** give him five instead. He may be the best guitarist we've heard so far but he nearly stole my girlfriend!

NEXT!

Things start to go weird after that. One kid plays a Spanish flamenco tune, another breaks out a banjo and then we wait around while another takes thirty-five minutes just to tune up! By the time **CHARLES GRAHAM** steps on the stage I'm thinking about giving up and going to Tahiti to sell tea towels.

Luckily **CHARLES** isn't bad. He's not good either, but that's not the point. By the time he's finished it's between him and **SAM LUTHER**. **JOSH** wants **SAM** because he's the better guitar player. **CLAUDIA** wants **SAM** because she's crazy. I want **CHARLES** because I'm not sharing the stage with **SAM**. In the end, as lead singer, I decide I have three votes and we go for **CHARLES**. **JOSH** and **CLAUDIA** aren't happy, but what can they do?

CLAUDIA storms off without saying goodbye. What's got into her? If anyone should be huffy it's me — she's got my prom ticket! Which reminds me, the band may be back on track, but if I want to get to the prom I'll need a ticket for myself. I call a band rehearsal for tomorrow with **JOSH** and **CHARLES**, and head for home.

I grab a hot dog on the way, which was a good idea because Mum made her Broctastic Broccoli Hash for dinner. It looks exactly the same as the Broccolicious Broccoli Bake, only with more broccoli. Apparently it's to cheer up **ELLIE** because she didn't get into the orchestra. Mr Burchester, the music teacher, said she needed more practice. Well, if she needs more practice, I need more ear plugs and Broctastic Broccoli Hash isn't going to cheer anyone up, except for maybe a rabbit. I give **ELLIE** one of my emergency chocolate bars to try and make her feel better.

After pushing my dinner around my plate for a bit, I make my excuses and come upstairs to write this. What with the extra ticket, the limo hire, the tuxedo hire and everything else, I'm going to need quite a bit more money for this whole prom thing. There's no way Mum and Dad are going to just give it to me . . . and I need to sort the cash so that I already had it this morning to buy the extra ticket before they sell out.

I'm going to have to do some chores. Lots of chores. I'm going to have to be like Chore Man, the world's worst super hero. So, diary, are you listening?

This morning I offered to do all the **chores** Mum and Dad want if I get the cash for a prom ticket and all the other stuff I'll need along the way. While I'm at it, I ran after **CLAUDIA** to find out why she was so angry with me after the band auditions.

Come on, diary,
I know you can do this!
Show me the money!

THURSDAY

When I wake up this morning there are two prom tickets on my desk and a pile of cash. It looks like I've been given six years' worth of pocket money or something — you won't hear me complaining! Then I get a bit confused by the TWO tickets. There should only be one, shouldn't there? CLAUDIA should have the other. Maybe I got really generous with my newfound cash and bought a spare just in case! **It's what rich people do.** Before you know it I'll be wearing trainers once then throwing them away!

When I get downstairs Mum is smiling at me. This makes me suspicious. Mum hasn't smiled for about eight months. **Maybe it's wind.** Then I notice that Dad's smiling at me too. **They can't BOTH have wind, can they?** We have been eating a lot of broccoli . . .

As I'm eating my breakfast Dad says he's really impressed with my new maturity and I start to get REALLY worried. What is he talking about? When I stand up to leave for school I find out. Before I can pull on my coat, Dad stops me and points behind me.

Pinned to the fridge is a list of **chores** that's longer than an award winner's thank you speech. Right at the bottom is **MY signature**. I must look puzzled because Mum explains,

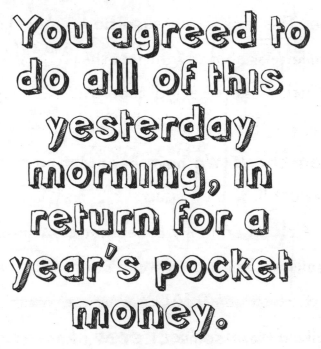

You agreed to do all of this yesterday morning, in return for a year's pocket money.

Dad chuckles. 'We thought you were ill or something.'

I take a closer look. Loads of **chores**,
divided into daily, weekly and monthly columns
are written on the list. What was I thinking?

There are some **chores** I know how to
do, like sweep the floors and clean the car.
But with others I don't even know where to

begin! **Apparently** I agreed to cook dinner once a week. **Are they sure about that?** So long as they don't mind eating burnt toast I guess it might work . . .

And how on earth am I supposed to change a lightbulb? They may as well have put 'perform heart surgery' or 'build a Porsche out of belly button fluff' on there too!

I'm about to say something, when I remember the prom tickets and the cash. I'm going to need all of it if I want to be Prom King. So I keep my mouth closed, check what I'm supposed to be doing this morning and get to work. It'll be worth it. I hope.

Mum hands me a basket of washing to fold

and Dad tells me I have to wash up all the breakfast stuff and put it away too. As I'm washing my cereal bowl I vow to eat my COCO SNAPS straight from the packet from now on!

By the time I get to school I'm fifteen minutes late for registration. I try to explain why to Mrs Johnson but she's not listening. I give **CLAUDIA** a wave but she doesn't wave back. In fact, she gives me the nastiest look I've ever seen. What's going on?

At break time **JOSH** fills me in. **CLAUDIA** is angry because I didn't ask her to audition for System of the Future last night. Apparently she'd brought along some music and was going to borrow one of our guitars but when I asked her to take down scores instead it was the final straw. At the end of the auditions I ran after her to find out what was wrong . . . and we had a __massive__ argument.

Apparently I brought up the whole buying her a prom ticket thing and she was so mad she said she wouldn't come with me and threw it back in my face. I guess that would explain why I still have two tickets. According to **JOSH**, now **CLAUDIA**'s decided to go to the prom with **BRAD RADLEY** instead because he just so happened to have a spare. Or he got his dad to print another one off, more likely!

I didn't even know **CLAUDIA** could play guitar, let alone that she'd want to audition for my band. Perhaps I should have paid a bit more attention. I think about using the diary to put things right tonight, but the audition was yesterday and the diary can only change things on the day they happen. I guess I've just got to rely on my natural charm and brilliant good looks to win her back. Nothing to worry about there then . . .

Later that afternoon, **BRAD** makes a big show of handing in his nomination papers for Prom King. It's like he's rubbing my nose in it. First he wangles a date with my (kind of) girlfriend and then he gets nominated for Prom King first. **CLAUDIA**'s been nominated for Prom Queen too. This day is turning into a total

I need to get nominated by tomorrow or I may as well disguise myself as a camel and emigrate to Egypt.

It shouldn't be a problem, all I need is two votes from people in my year, and there's two other members of System of the Future – if they both nominate me then I'm home and dry. I'll get them to do it at rehearsal tonight.

After lunch we have P.E. with Mr Bucklestrap. He's decided that it would be 'fun' to teach us all how to play American Football in honour of **BLAKE**'s visit. Which sounds cool, but it turns out American Football is nothing like <u>normal</u> football.

For one thing they wear helmets and shoulder pads! **Seriously,** if a sport needs **THAT** kind of protection it shouldn't be called a sport, it should be called **survival**.

We don't have any of the equipment, but that doesn't stop Mr Bucklestrap making us play anyway. While the girls learn cheerleading skills, I get barged and battered from one end of the playing field to the other. In the end I spend most of the time trying to avoid the ball so that I won't become a target, but even that doesn't work! The ball only has to head in my general direction and all of a sudden I'm at the bottom of a mountain of kids! By the time we're finished **I'm bruised and battered all over** and my shoulder is really sore.

After P.E. it's science. I ask if I can visit the school nurse about my shoulder but Mr Lilley remembers my long trip to the toilet last time and thinks I'm just trying to skive again! By the time I get home my shoulder has seized up so much I can barely lift my fork to my mouth. Which is a relief, as Mum's made her **Best Broccoli Cheeseburgers.** Without the burgers. It tastes like **an accident at a cheese factory** so the fact I have an excuse not to eat it is a **bonus!** Before I head to band practice Dad points at the **chore list.** I have to wash up. I spend the next twenty minutes trying to chisel cheesy **broccoli burgers** off a frying pan with a spatula. It's like trying to **break into Fort Knox with a teaspoon.**

When I've finally finished I grab my guitar and I'm heading out of the door when Dad stops me. Where do I think I'm going? Have I forgotten about the baby's scan? Apparently the whole family are going to the hospital this evening to find out whether Mum's expecting a boy or a girl. I'd forgotten all about it.

Dad asks me what's more important — meeting my new brother or sister, or my band? Apparently 'band' is the WRONG answer. I'm frogmarched to the car where Mum and ELLIE are waiting. I make Dad promise to drop me off at school for practice afterwards, though, and he agrees. I send JOSH a text to tell him I'm running late.

The car takes ages to start. Every time Dad turns the key it sounds like **an asthmatic gorilla.** Finally it judders into life and we chug to the hospital. Now that **ELLIE** is learning the violin, she's abandoned **Charlie Dimples** and has got really into classical music, so we spend the whole trip listening to **Radio Boring, the dullest radio station ever.** To make matters worse, she mimes playing the violin along to the music, elbowing me in the eye accidentally on purpose every time. **As if having a sore shoulder wasn't enough!**

When we finally get to hospital we spend fifteen minutes looking at a fluffy grey cloud on a screen while everyone **oohs** and **aahs.** I can't see what all the fuss is about — have

they never seen the sky before? Turns out
the cloud is actually my baby brother
or sister, but he (or she) is in the wrong
position for us to find out which it is.

<u>Brilliant</u> – the whole trip was a waste of time anyway!

As Mum and Dad are chatting to the nurse, my shoulder starts to hurt again. I borrow the scanner to see if I can find out what's wrong. No sooner is the wand in my hand than it starts to beep like a dalek at a disco. At first I think that this must mean my shoulder is seriously hurt, but apparently it means I've broken the machine. Oops. The nurse goes <u>ballistic</u> and marches me out of her office, which is a harsh way to treat a potential patient if you ask me!

Mum and Dad are really embarrassed and Dad refuses to drop me off at school like he promised to. They've decided I am grounded.

This is a

I try to text **JOSH**, but Dad confiscates my phone, then he confiscates my guitar. Apparently I need to be taught a lesson.

I have to fix this!

If I hadn't hurt my shoulder playing **stupid** American Football then none of this would have happened. I need my guitar if I'm going to have any chance of winning back **CLAUDIA** and being voted Prom King. Luckily I have a diary that can make that happen.

So, diary, I didn't play American Football. That way my shoulder wouldn't have hurt, I wouldn't have used the scanner at the hospital and I wouldn't have been grounded and had my guitar stolen – **got it?** My whole prom depends on **you.**

FRIDAY

When I woke up this morning my guitar was still standing against the wall and my shoulder wasn't hurting anymore. Result! Now all I had to do was get nominated for Prom King, win back CLAUDIA and my life would be back on track.

When I got downstairs, I put my new plan to dodge the washing up into action. Instead of taking a bowl for breakfast, I simply poured some milk into the cereal box and dug in with a spoon.

Result! Washing up halved in an instant! Dad wasn't too impressed that I'd finished all the COCO SNAPS though and **ELLIE** said she thought it was 'gross'. Which we all know is **ELLIE**-speak for 'I'm just jealous 'cos I didn't think of it first!'

Unfortunately my plan backfired when the milk soaked through the bottom of the packet and the whole lot exploded onto the floor. Oops. It took me twice as long to clear it up as it would have done to do the washing up, but that's not the point. All geniuses have setbacks.

I was about to head for school when Mum pointed to the chore list on the fridge. It was bin day and I had to take the bag from the kitchen bin to the wheelie bin out in the front. Everyone hates that job. It's worse than collecting bogies from a snotty elephant.

As I got close, the smell struck me. The kitchen bin smelled worse than a dung beetle's laundry basket.

I grabbed a peg and shoved it on my nose. It didn't help. I could STILL smell week-old broccoli bin juice. I had to give the bag a little wiggle to get it out, which only unlocked MORE smells. Then, as I struggled to open the door, bin juice started to leak out of the bottom of the bag and down my trousers like zombie slime. I couldn't get outside soon enough and I nearly barfed as I chucked the bag into the wheelie bin.

When I went back inside, the bin juice smell came with me. Mum said I couldn't go to school smelling like that — result! I could stay at home! Apparently that wasn't quite what she had in mind. She sent me back upstairs to get changed. Unfortunately my other school trousers were in the wash, so Mum said I could wear 'something sensible'. Which we all know is mum-speak for 'whatever you want.' Besides, she was going for a nap, EVEN THOUGH SHE'D ONLY JUST WOKEN UP, so she'd never know. You snooze, you lose! I picked out some of my favourite clothes. If today was the day I was going to be nominated for Prom King, I could at least dress the part. I picked out a baseball cap, T-shirt and jeans and made my way to school.

Because of the whole bin juice thing I arrived at school late again. And when Mrs

Johnson saw what I was wearing she got really angry. She said I'd been late nearly every day this week and that I needed to buck my ideas up. I tried to explain that Mum and Dad had turned me into their personal slave, but she wasn't listening. Typical.

Then, JOSH leaned over and said

What happened to your nose?

What did he mean? He took a picture on his phone and showed me. My nose was bright red where I'd clipped the peg on it. I looked like Rudolph the Red-nosed Reindeer . . . after he'd just smacked into a chimney!

Mrs Johnson sent me home to get changed into my school uniform. I tried to explain about the bin juice and the washing but she said that unless I was back here in half an hour in 'correct uniform' then I shouldn't come back at all. For a moment I tried to figure out where the catch was in that. Not coming back at all didn't sound so bad. Then I remembered the Prom King nomination – I had to be here. So I ran home, pulled on my bin-juice trousers – because they were at least DRY – and ran back again.

When I got back into class Mrs Johnson STILL wasn't happy. Everyone in the room made a big show about coughing and spluttering and holding their noses. BRAD RADLEY opened a window and pretended to be sick out of it. <u>Oh, come on!</u> I didn't smell **THAT** bad. Then I had a sniff of myself and nearly passed out. OK. Maybe I did.

Mrs Johnson's eyes were watering. I don't know if it was because she was so angry she was crying — I've seen that happen to teachers! — or because of the smell. She sent me to see the school receptionist in case she had some spare trousers.

The only trousers she had were two sizes too small. And I had to pay for them! I bought them anyway, using up some of my prom money. Not only was I out of pocket, I was going to have to suck my tummy in for the rest of the day. It wasn't even ten o'clock and my day was already a

DOUBLE DISASTER!

By the time my trousers were sorted it was time for break. **BRAD RADLEY** was standing by the noticeboard everyone passes on the way out to the playground. I knew something was up because he was grinning like a madman at an axe factory. I was right to be worried.

BRAD had made up a poster of . . . me. The photo must have been from yesterday, and suddenly I realised why my shoulder wasn't aching. In the poster I was shaking my pom-poms with the cheerleaders. **BRAD** had written

Meet Your (Cheer) Leader

at the bottom. Not exactly Prom King material.

Meet Your (Cheer) Leader

Everyone was gathered round and laughing. **BRAD** pointed at me and said

Shake your pom-poms, Fin

and I couldn't take it any more. I tore down the poster and threw it in the bin before storming off.

BLAKE ROMNEY caught up with me and explained that yesterday Mr Bucklestrap had given me a choice. I could either play American Football with the boys or practice cheerleading with the girls. I had chosen cheerleading! Thanks, diary.

BLAKE tried to cheer me up. He said that I'd actually been pretty funky and had shown off some crazy moves. All the girls loved it! Well, I didn't care about all the girls! I wanted to be Prom King not Cheerleading Queen. **BLAKE** insisted that in America some of the best cheerleaders were actually guys, but I wasn't listening. I'm starting to remember why I stopped using this diary — things never go according to plan.

At least I could rely on my band to cheer me up. Only I couldn't! Our new guitarist **CHARLES** was really angry with me and **JOSH** was taking his side. They were annoyed that I hadn't turned up for practice. I didn't understand — the diary should have fixed it that even though I was late from the hospital visit, I'd have got there eventually. Besides I sent them a text to explain:

> Running late,
> be there soon!

JOSH showed me his phone. It said:

> Stunning gate.
> Bye bye loons!

My phone is so old the buttons have got sticky and the predictive text keeps going wrong. I need a new one, but there's no chance of that with all the cash I'm splashing on this prom business.

I explained about my dodgy phone. **JOSH** said they'd waited for a bit, but they'd given up after an hour. That was probably just before I made it back from the hospital. I apologised and said we could probably squeeze in a rehearsal before the prom audition tonight. **JOSH** seemed to cheer up at that, but **CHARLES** huffed and said he 'supposed so'

and then he left. I hadn't even got the chance to ask him to sign my nomination paper.

JOSH signed anyway, but that didn't solve my problem. I needed two nominations. Who else was I going to ask?

The answer came at lunchtime. I was sitting at a table by myself looking at my bangers and mash when **SAM LUTHER** came to join me. Normally I would have told him to go away, but I couldn't be bothered. I was feeling too low. The band thing was bad, the cheerleading thing was awful, the Prom King nomination thing was <u>a total disaster</u> and to top it all my trousers were so tight I couldn't risk eating another mouthful of my lunch in case they sprang open like a mummy's casket. It wasn't fair.

SAM sympathised and said he was sure it would all work out in the end. It was then that I had an idea. I whipped out my nomination paper and a pen and asked **SAM** to be my second nominee for Prom King. **SAM** smiled and took the pen, but then he stopped. He said he'd only sign if I promised he could play a song with me at the prom. He was really gutted that we hadn't chosen him to join System of the Future, and he really wanted us to perform together.

Share the stage with **SAM** in return for the chance to be Prom King. Was it worth it?

<u>Of course it was!</u> I promised **SAM** a starring role and he signed on the dotted line.

I was SO excited I ran straight to hand in my nomination paper. As I was heading back to class I bumped into **CLAUDIA**. She complimented me on my cheerleading skills and I complimented her on finding another date for the prom. She shook her head. Apparently it was all off — she wasn't going with **BRAD RADLEY** any more. My heart skipped a beat . . . was I in with another chance?

Turns out I wasn't. She had decided

to go with **LUCY** instead. She said boys were nothing but trouble and it would be fun to party with the girls instead.

This was a

If **CLAUDIA** was going with **LUCY**, she couldn't go with me. There had to be a way to fix this . . . I needed to get **LUCY** a date! If she had a date for prom, then **CLAUDIA** would be free to go with me.

JOSH, CHARLES and I finally managed to sneak in a quick rehearsal before the Prom Band auditions and considering we'd never played together before we were pretty good.

The audition was taking place in the school hall. There were only two other bands auditioning, not that you could call them bands. Mr Burchester has a string quartet called **On the Fiddle.** They only play classical music – <u>no chance!</u> And **CLARE DALSTON** from another class in our year was there with her state-of-the-art synthesiser. Everyone knows synthesisers can't rock! **System of the Future** were **the only choice!**

Mr Burchester's band was so boring they'd send insomniacs to sleep and **CLARE**'s synthesiser got stuck on demo mode so we just heard 'Frère Jaques' on continuous loop for <u>fifteen minutes</u> until she managed to turn it off.

Then System of the Future started our audition. We sounded great! So great I decided to try one of my more ambitious dance moves. A little too ambitious, as it turns out. As I was doing a high kick I heard a loud 'POP' and my trousers fell down. Brilliant. No rock star looks good with his trousers round his ankles! Thank goodness I was wearing my best pants. As I waddled off stage BLAKE and the committee told everyone they'd let us know on Monday.

This was a

Everything had all been going so well until the whole trouser-popping thing.

CLAUDIA's date with **BRAD** was off, I was on the nominations for Prom King — if I could just make sure System of the Future were picked for Prom Band and then find **LUCY** a date then everything would be going my way.

So, diary, are you listening? You need to fix this.

I didn't spill bin juice down my trousers this morning, and I didn't go to school smelling like a troll's toilet! My entire life depends on you!

SATURDAY

When I woke up this morning the pile of money on my desk looked a little bit larger and the too-small trousers I'd bought yesterday were gone. It looked like the diary had worked! To make sure, I grabbed my school trousers from the washing basket and sniffed them for bin juice. Unfortunately ELLIE walked past at just the wrong moment.

Mum! Fin's sniffing his trousers again!

What does she mean '<u>again</u>'? Anyway, the good news is, if my trousers didn't pop open yesterday the audition should be in the bag. **Prom King** and **Prom Band** here I come!

After breakfast — which Mum insisted I eat from a bowl — **ELLIE** cranked up her violin practice. Seriously, she's really trying to annoy me today! If the tune she's playing is called 'Screechy, Screechy, Screechy' then she's aceing it every time. I have to get out of the house before Mum or Dad can get me started on the **chore list** so I grab some money and head to the shop for some sweets.

As I'm trying to decide between Whizzy Worms and Chocolate Chewbits, I hear a voice behind me.

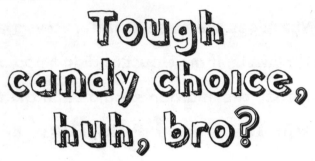

Tough candy choice, huh, bro?

It's **BLAKE**. He calls sweets 'candy' for some reason. It's another one of those American things. In the end I buy both and we get chatting. I ask him about the audition last night. He winks and says, 'No comment!', which we all know is **BLAKE**-speak for 'It's in the bag!'

Result!

I'm in such a good mood I invite him back to my place to share my candy — he's got me doing it now — and play a game of **DEATH SQUADRON**.

It turns out **BLAKE**'s really good at **DEATH SQUADRON** and just as he's killing me for the fifth time he asks if I want to play **DEATH SQUADRON: ANNIHILATION**. Do I? Of course I do, but it's only out in America. But then I twig. **BLAKE**'s from America! Aces! **BLAKE** pulls a copy out of his bag. I told you this kid was cool!

DEATH SQUADRON: ANNIHILATION is as good as the internet says it is. We spend the next hour playing it nonstop. As we play **BLAKE** fills me in on all the things he's doing this week to get ready for the prom. I listen really hard — **BLAKE**'s done this before and I want to make sure I don't miss a thing! If I'm going to be made Prom King I have to do this right.

By the time he's finished I know I need a tuxedo, a haircut, flowers for my date, a limo . . . I'm just starting to worry about money when **BLAKE** offers to give me a lift in the limo he's hiring.

Double result!

I knew he was a good guy.

BLAKE's also getting some dance lessons. He wants to look his best when he struts his stuff on the dancefloor. That sounds like a good idea to me too, but before I can agree, Mum, who just so happens to bustle in with biscuits as he's saying all this, tells me not to worry about that, she has a plan. Which we all know is Mum-speak for 'Start stressing, kid, this isn't going to end well.' Before I can say anything, though, **BLAKE** has zapped me with a laser beam and I'm back in the game. We must be making a bit of noise because then **ELLIE** comes in to tell us to keep it down.

What a cheek! She's the one who's been polluting the world with her violin for the last week! But when she claps eyes on **BLAKE**, she goes a bit quiet and tells us not to worry about it. Three levels later we go downstairs to get a *soda* — that's **BLAKE**-speak for 'can of pop', by the way — and **ELLIE** appears again, following him round like a puppy.

Just when I think things can't get any worse, she goes to get her violin so she can play **BLAKE** a song. This is too much! Before she comes back, **BLAKE** makes some excuse about needing to 'bounce' — whatever that means — and I try to get his copy of **DEATH SQUADRON: ANNIHILATION** out of my console. I'm in such a rush that I panic and snap it in two. It's a

The only copy of **DEATH SQUADRON: ANNIHILATION** in the country and I've just broken it! **BLAKE**'s face goes as white as a sheet. He makes his excuses and leaves.

That's just brilliant! I wouldn't be surprised if he bans me from the prom altogether for that! There's no chance he'll let me perform, let alone be Prom King. This is all **ELLIE**'s fault. If she hadn't been so weird none of this would have happened. I tell **ELLIE** her violin playing sucks more than a granny with a throat lozenge. She goes all quiet and heads downstairs. Mum spots her and says she's off to the shops and 'needs a hand', which we all know is mum-speak for 'Boss you up and down the aisles.' I smile. I'm glad she found **ELLIE** first!

Serves her right!

Turns out I had spoken too soon because just then Dad finds me and asks me to 'give him a hand' too. He's organised a surprise baby shower for Mum and all of her friends are coming over this afternoon for a picnic in the garden. I'm just starting to wonder what this has got to do with me when he gives me a list of jobs. He's getting very good at this. Dad's got a longer list than Santa Claus!

I spend the next hour moving tables, chairs and picnic blankets out into the garden while long-lost relatives arrive to tell me I've grown since they last saw me. Well, it'd be a bit weird if I'd shrunk! We blow up balloons, hang streamers and ferry enough crisps and sausage rolls outside to feed an army of Girl Guides.

When Mum and **ELLIE** arrive back everyone shouts

SURPRISE!

and Mum looks genuinely shocked, which is nice. Suddenly everyone is talking about babies and nappies and milk and I realise it's time to make my excuses and leave. But Aunty Suzie stops me. She thinks it would be nice if I 'joined in'. Which we all know is aunty-speak for 'Play along or there's no Christmas present for you, sunshine.'

I suppose Dad has organised some quite good party games. First everyone votes as to whether they think the baby's a boy or a girl, then we play 'name the baby' and Mum and Dad reveal they're thinking of calling the

103

baby Spencer. I can't quite believe my ears. Spencer **Spencer? That's worse than Monty!** <u>The poor kid</u>. I'm sure everyone else agrees with me, but they're too polite to say so.

After the name game we play 'Pin the Dummy on the Baby' which sounds cruel but is actually quite fun, then we are all timed putting a nappy on a dolly. It takes me nearly three minutes — who knew those things would be so complicated? **ELLIE** does it in 23 seconds and wins a prize.

What do people expect? It's her doll! To be honest I don't mind her winning. If she wants to prove she's best at changing nappies that's fine by me. She can do every single one when the new baby arrives!

FIN SPENCER'S RIGHT ROYAL RULE 4
SOME GAMES ARE TRAPS

Then **ELLIE** makes everyone a badge with the badge-maker she got for Christmas. She makes one for me that says 'Big Bro', which is pretty cool, I guess. Then Dad breaks out a load of baby food and we have to taste it to guess what it is. I'm just relieved it's not broccoli so get really stuck in. I'm just polishing off my third pot of Chicken Supreme when **something terrible happens.**

BRAD RADLEY arrives at Mum's baby shower.

It turns out my mum and his mum have got talking at school parents' evenings so Dad invited her along to the baby shower. I want the ground to open up and swallow me whole. **BRAD RADLEY**, my Prom King rival, is watching me eat baby food.

However I have nothing to worry about because before long he's forced to 'join in' too! Nice one, Aunty Suzie. Surprisingly, with no one else around to show off to, **BRAD** can actually be quite a nice guy. We end up on the same team for baby bottle bowling and each score a strike!

Just as I'm thinking things are going OK again, Dad brings out baby photos. There's one of everybody at the party and we have to guess who is who.

Aunty Suzie points at one of the pictures and says

That's Fin! He's still got wonky eyebrows!

Everyone laughs. What is she talking about? I do not have wonky eyebrows! Annoyingly **BRAD** and his mum have to go before we find out which of the photos is him. But it's been good spending time with him away from school. We may be Prom King rivals, but it's nice to know we can still be friends. Sort of.

After they leave everybody moves onto baby stories. At first I'm worried.

There's this one story Mum and Dad love to tell about me as a baby. Apparently I pooed in the bath. It gets longer and longer every time — the story, not the poo — and everyone finds it hilarious except me. Just as I'm thinking they may have forgotten it, **ELLIE** brings it up. I could kill her!

She looks at me in a way that says

In your face, loser boy!

As Mum and Dad are laughing about how they scooped the poo out with a fishing net, I sneak over to the badge-making machine. **ELLIE** has had it in for me all day and it's time she was taught a lesson. Her **stupid violin-playing** made me break **BLAKE**'s **DEATH SQUADRON: ANNIHILATION** and now she's embarrassing me in front of everyone. I decide to make her a special badge of her very own – a Silly Little Sister badge.

When I hand it over **ELLIE** starts to cry. Mum and Dad aren't impressed. Nor is anyone else. I get sent to my room.

Which is kind of a  result as I don't have
to do any of the tidying up. But it's also kind
of a

DISASTER!

as they confiscate my TV.

This whole day has been **ELLIE**'s fault.

I need you to fix this, diary — OK?

I didn't rush when I took out **DEATH
SQUADRON: ANNIHILATION** and I didn't
make **ELLIE** a badge, or if I did it said
'Super Sis' on it or something. Instead
I told everyone her baby story about how she
was so scared of the vacuum cleaner she hit
it with a brush. There! See how she likes it!

SUNDAY

When I got downstairs this morning **ELLIE** was wearing a badge that said 'Super Sis' on the front and I was happier than a donkey in a carrot shop. It turns out I had basically been **FINCREDIBLE** yesterday. I'd helped out and tidied all day and no one seemed to know anything about the real badge I'd made for **ELLIE**. For the first time in ages Mum and Dad were pleased with me, my TV was back in my bedroom and Mum said that I really deserved the 'special surprise' she had in store for me later.

I was getting a surprise? Cool!
I started trying to work out what it might be.

1 New **X-WING** T-shirt

2 Advance copy of **DEATH SQUADRON: ANNIHILATION**

3 A year's supply of chocolate ice cream

It might even be all three!

Then I had a brainwave. There were loads of plastic bowls and spoons left over from the party yesterday. Before anyone could have their breakfast cereal I went to fetch them and made everybody use them instead of the normal ones. Plastic bowls and spoons could be thrown away, which meant no washing up! **I am a genius!** These genius ideas are happening **so regularly** people should probably start calling me **EINSTEIN SPENCER**. I'd better not suggest it to Mum and Dad just in case they give the name to the new baby instead!

As I'm munching through my COCO SNAPS I send **BLAKE** a text message just to check that the diary has worked on his broken game too, but it doesn't go as planned. What I thought I wrote was:

> Hope your Death
> Squadron game is OK!

but what my dodgy phone sent was:

> Hope your breath
> squawking brain is OK!

I hate predictive text. **BLAKE** sent me a really confused message back. I think he thought 'breath squawking' might be some sort of weird British slang. In the end I gave him a call. The **DEATH SQUADRON** game was fine — result!

After I did the tidying up from breakfast — i.e. chucked everything in the bin — I prepared for a long day of relaxing in my room. I needed to figure out everything I still needed for the prom. Unfortunately Dad **had other ideas.** He pointed to the **chore list** on the fridge. Apparently I was supposed to be mowing the lawn and weeding the garden. I couldn't believe it — I thought Sunday was supposed to be a day of rest? **Not if you're FIN SPENCER.**

I was about to start complaining when Mum said, 'Now you don't want to undo all the good work you did yesterday, do you?' Which we all know is mum-speak for 'Suck it up, loser boy, or I'll confiscate your cash!' So I got changed into some old clothes and trudged outside. **At least I had Mum's surprise to look forward to later.**

I started by weeding the garden. Or at least I thought that's what I was doing. I went round with a black bin bag tearing up anything that looked ugly or dead. When Mum came out to see how I was doing she nearly had a fit. Apparently I'd 'ransacked the perennials', whatever that means! How was I supposed to know? Everything looked the same! Mum snatched away the bin bag and told me to concentrate on mowing the lawn instead. Result! I'm starting to realise that if you do a job badly people ask you to stop doing it. Do a job well and they find you another one. Doing jobs badly is where it's at, people!

FIN SPENCER'S RIGHT ROYAL RULE 5

DO A JOB BADLY,
NEVER GET ASKED
TO DO IT AGAIN!

Mowing the lawn was actually quite fun. Not least because it drowned out **ELLIE**'s violin practice. The only problem is that going up and down, up and down gets really boring after a while. To liven things up I decided to write my name in the grass. When I'd finished **F — I — N** was spelled out in huge letters across the lawn. **A beautiful sight!**

Turns out Dad was watching from the bathroom window . . .

At first I thought he was going to shout at me, but he actually wanted a go himself. He spelled out **D — A — D** right next to my name. **The only one who didn't think it was funny was Mum.** She made us mow over it and then took the lawnmower off us. Apparently we 'couldn't be trusted'. Which we all know is mum-speak for 'You're a pair of idiots!' Still, it's another job I never have to do again! Result!

The good news is that despite my gardening mishaps Mum was **still** happy for me to have my surprise. We hop in the car and I reckon we're off for a trip to the shops. Unfortunately the car has other ideas! Every time Mum turns the key it splutters like **an angry teacher.** After a few more tries the car **finally** gets going and we head towards the shops . . .

. . . and drive straight past them.

I'm confused. **Where are we going?** Mum won't tell me. She says it would spoil the surprise.

Before long we arrive in Aunty Suzie's street and now I'm more worried than **a carrot at a bunny farm.** As we park the car, Mum explains. Apparently Aunty Suzie is a ballroom dancer in her spare time, and when Mum heard **BLAKE ROMNEY**

and me talking about dancing at the prom she thought it would be fun if she asked Aunty Suzie to give me a lesson.

Fun! How is spending the afternoon dancing with your aunty fun? It feels like I'm about to audition for Strictly Come Nightmare! Frankly I'd rather pickle my nose pickings.

I try to persuade Mum to reverse off the drive, but it's too late. Aunty Suzie is at the door wearing a ballroom dress that makes her look like a cross between an American wrestler and a Christmas tree. Help!

I spend the next two hours learning to do the foxtrot. I keep standing on Aunt Suzie's toes so she suggests trying the cha cha cha instead. I explain that I don't want to choo choo choo or whatever it's called, that we won't be dancing to THIS sort of music at the prom, we'll be dancing to modern stuff.

Mum looks a bit put out but Aunty Suzie says she gets the picture and starts to rifle through her LPs for 'Something a little bit more recent.' Which is aunty-speak for 'Something from this century'. Finally she finds a record and pops it on.

For a moment I don't know what's more offensive — the music coming out of the speakers, or the moves my aunty is trying to bust. She looks like a trout on a trampoline! Apparently she's doing something called 'disco' and it's what all the young people danced to back in ancient times, when nobody had TVs . . . or taste!

Then she starts to do this weird thing with her arms. You have to throw them about like you're having a fit! Mum tells me to join in, and soon we're both having fits!

As the music reaches a climax Aunty Suzie gets a little carried away and she bashes me in the face with a runaway hand! Ouch!

Aunty Suzie turns off the music and is really apologetic, but my eye is already starting to swell up. She fetches a bag of peas from the freezer, wraps them in a tea towel and plonks it on my face. Perfect. At least it puts an end to my disco nightmare!

When we get home my eye isn't getting any better. ELLIE has a look and says, 'Oh, you poor thing', which we all know is ELLIE-speak for, 'Ha! Ha! Ha! In your face!' Mum thinks I'm going to have a black eye in the morning.

This can't be happening! This is the most important week of my life. Prom Kings don't have black eyes.

I just want to chill out and watch some TV, but Mum and Dad have other ideas. They want to watch a bit more of Das Kop Shau. I leave them discussing more Swedish baby names and head upstairs.

When I look in the mirror, my eye is redder than a *baboon's bottom!* I can't go to school like this. **The diary needs to fix it.** It helped with the bin juice, being nice to **ELLIE** and getting my money back, so I'm feeling confident.

OK, diary. I didn't go to see Aunty Suzie today, I refused to do any of my **chores** so Mum cancelled the surprise. I don't know how to **foxtrot, cha cha cha or disco.** I don't need to know how to dance anyway. I'll be too busy rocking everybody else with my band.

MONDAY

When I wake up this morning I run straight to the mirror and my eye is back to normal. **Phew!** My journey to Prom King Royalty is back on track *and* I didn't spend my Sunday boogying with my aunt! **Thank you, diary!**

When I get downstairs, though, things aren't as rosy. Mum and Dad are **really angry** with me because I didn't do my **chores** properly yesterday. They've added them to the list for this week so now I have even more to do. **I didn't think that was possible!**

I'm in a rush to get to school because this morning we find out which band made it to the prom! I try to convince Mum and Dad to eat out of plastic bowls again. But no such luck, AND **ELLIE** insists on having pancakes so I've got even more than usual to wash up. I swear she does these things on purpose! She's more annoying than a toddler with a trumpet.

I get to school just as the bell goes and manage to sneak in a quick chat with **BLAKE ROMNEY**. The good news is the Prom Committee have decided that System of the Future can play at the prom

— result! The bad news is they've decided that everyone else can play too. Apparently the prom is all about everyone pulling together to make it a special night and that should be the case with the bands too! Brilliant. I'll be sharing a stage with Mr Burchester's violin monstrosity and a synthesiser-playing loser. I'll just have to blast them so far off stage they'll be playing a prom on Pluto.

I tell **CHARLES** and **JOSH** the good news and arrange some more rehearsals.

At break time Mr Finch pins the Prom King and Prom Queen nominations to his door. There are four Prom King nominees, one each from the other two classes and two from mine. The two from my class are me, **FIN SPENCER** . . . and **BRAD RADLEY**. I thought **BLAKE** might have wanted to have a go, but he said he'd have the chance to be king of loads of proms when he got back to America so he decided to let a Brit have a turn! See? Told you he was a nice guy.

CLAUDIA is on the Prom Queen list along with two other girls. They don't stand a chance. Everybody loves **CLAUDIA**.

I just need to make sure she's **MY** prom queen — starting with making sure she's my date to the prom, not **LUCY**'s.

Luckily this genius has a plan. I'm going to write **LUCY** a poem, slip it into her schoolbag and pretend it's from **JOSH**. That way **LUCY** will fall instantly in love with **JOSH**, drop **CLAUDIA** and I can step in to the rescue. Good, huh?

I'm just starting to enjoy the fact that everything is going my way when

strikes. I head outside to find **BRAD RADLEY** grinning at me. His face is plastered all over the outside of the building.

It's like I'm living in some kind of nightmare! It turns out that he got his dad to print some posters and now he's put them up everywhere. They say:

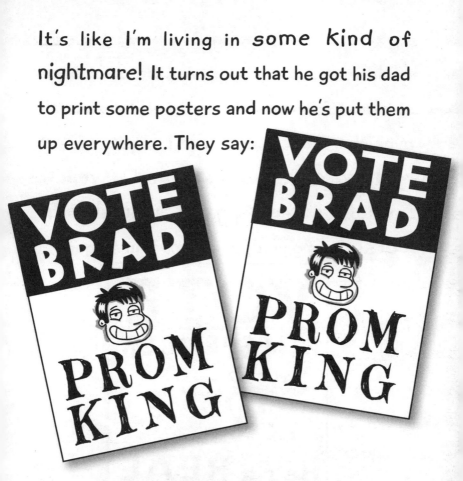

I am about to complain about how unfair this all is when **BRAD** himself comes up to tell me that he's made some for me too. Aw, I knew, deep down, he was a nice guy . . .

Wrong!

He's used my baby photo! He must have swiped it from the baby shower, because all over the school there are posters of me wearing a frilly nappy and a yellow bonnet, and sucking my dummy! Even worse, he's given me a campaign slogan:

VOTE
FIN SPENCER
He's a REAL DUMMY!

This is war! I rip them all down and stuff them in the bin. I'll have to make my own posters for tomorrow. **I'm in a really bad mood** and it's not helped when **SAM LUTHER** comes to find me. He's really pleased that System of the Future are playing the prom. It means we'll get to perform together. At first I don't know what he's going on about and then I remember the promise I made when he said he'd nominate me. There's **no way** that's going to happen! I don't tell him that, though, instead I just nod and smile and say 'Sure thing', which we all know is Fin-speak for 'Not in a million years!'

After break Mr Finch takes us for a lesson on online bullying. He's heard that it's on the rise and wants to make it clear that the school won't tolerate it. I'm with him on that, **I don't**

want to be bullied online or off line.
I try to tell him about **BRAD**'s smear campaign,
but I've binned all the posters and without
evidence he won't listen to me. <u>Typical</u>.

During lunch there is a meeting of the
Prom Committee. Now that they've got
the bands sorted they want to decide on a
theme. I suggest **'FIN SPENCER'**
but apparently the theme cannot be me. In
the end we settle on 'Movie Glamour', which
is close, I guess! Just before we head back
to class I put Operation Date **LUCY** into
action and slip the love poem I've written
into **LUCY**'s bag. I'm pretty pleased with
what I've come up with, and it also sounds
rubbish enough to have been written by
JOSH:

Darling Lucy P
Come to the prom
with Josh,
If you're still free,
I'll say yippee,
And even have
a wash!

Cupid, eat your heart out! After the meeting **BLAKE** and I walk back to class. I show him my prom checklist:

TUXEDO   next to do
LIMO   getting a lift with Blake
DATE   all in hand
HAIRCUT   to do
PROM KING   working on it
DANCING   let's not even go there

I tell him everything's going OK apart from the dancing. He says:

Have a look online, my fat friend, there's some dope stuff on there!

Good idea, **BLAKE**, I knew we were friends for a reason — but why's he calling me fat?

As I'm walking home, I see **CLAUDIA** and **LUCY** chatting. **LUCY** is holding the poem I wrote from **JOSH**. I can't wait to hear what she thinks so I walk a bit faster to get close enough to overhear. I wish I hadn't bothered. It's a disaster! She hates it. **LUCY** thinks **JOSH** sounds desperate. She and **CLAUDIA** both agree that they're glad they're not going with boys this year. Honestly!

I'll have to use the diary to fix it and think of something else.

Later when I get home I go straight upstairs and have a look online for some dance routines to practise. There's some guy spinning on his head, which looks cool but painful. Not to mention IMPOSSIBLE! There's another guy who seems like he'd give Michael Jackson a run for his money but really isn't my style. In the end I settle on copying a kid about my age who's worked out a routine to my favourite

X-WING song, 'Fighter Pilot'. Just as I'm getting into it **ELLIE** cranks up her violin. I run next door to tell her to give it up — she'll never get into an orchestra sounding like that! For once she actually listens and gives me a bit of peace and quiet — result!

After my dance practice, which actually goes pretty well even if I do say so myself, I decide I need a new look and book a posh haircut for tomorrow after school. It's going to cost me a fortune but it'll be worth it. Dance in the bag, haircut booked — my prom list is coming together like a jigsaw in an old people's home.

When I get downstairs, Dad's fiddling with his new camera again. He wants to take some practice shots of me, and I'm about to say no way when I remember I need a **Prom King** poster. If Dad takes a cool shot of me then I can use it for that. I strike a pose and Dad takes a picture.

FLASH!

He's turned the flash up so high I'm nearly blinded! I stagger backwards into the TV and can't see properly for an hour! **Back to the drawing board, Dad.**

Just as my eyes are recovering, Mum comes in from the shops. She tells me she's got all the things I need for dinner. I have no idea what she's talking about. She points at the list on the fridge. **Apparently it's my turn to cook!**

Fair enough. I just hope my family know

what they're letting themselves in for. Mum's got a recipe book and a whole greengrocer's worth of broccoli. Surprise surprise — I'm making Broccolicious Broccoli Bake!

Once I get started it's actually quite good fun and as I pop it in the oven I'm feeling pretty pleased with myself. I'm about to put the recipe book back on the shelf when it flips onto the 'Desserts' section. There's a recipe for cookies and it gives me an idea. I'm clearly a natural at this whole cooking thing, so instead of putting up posters why don't I make cookies to hand out tomorrow? That'd show **BRAD RADLEY** who the real Prom King is.

The only problem is that all the utensils are dirty from making the broccoli bake.

I can't be bothered to wash it all up **TWICE** so I decide to use the same mixing bowl and spoon. No one will ever know. I even find some icing pens left over from the baby shower. Result!

Mum and Dad are polite about the *broccoli bake* and say 'It's good for a first try.' Which we all know is parent-speak for 'You are a master chef! I bow down before you!'

I'm so exhausted after all that cooking that I'm ready for bed. Before I climb in, though, I need to fix the whole **LUCY** and **JOSH** date thing.

So, diary, I didn't write the poem, OK? I'll think of another genius plan in the morning.

TUESDAY

This morning started a little too early. About six hours too early, to be precise. I was in such a rush to get to bed last night that I forgot all about the cookies! The smoke from the oven set off the smoke alarms and Mum and Dad found themselves in the kitchen at one in the morning, flapping tea towels at the ceiling like hippies at a pagan ceremony. They were not impressed.

140

ELLIE managed to sleep through it. I guess compared to her violin-playing the smoke alarm sounded like a symphony.

Anyway, when I got down to the kitchen for breakfast Mum and Dad were bleary-eyed and angry, while **ELLIE** was grinning like an air hostess on holiday. I apologised to Mum and Dad and went to get the cookies from the side. OK, so they were a little burned and it was hard to ice them because they were so bumpy, but I was sure they'd taste great. I shoved them in my bag. My class were going to love them!

Before I could leave for school, though, I had a load more chores to do from the weekend. Mum wanted me to vacuum my room. That was harder than it sounded because I

141

hadn't actually seen the floor in three months. I threw everything onto the bed, found fifteen dirty plates and something that used to be a sausage roll under my desk, and spent the next twenty minutes choking in a dust cloud.

I was late to school again and Mrs Johnson said I was on my 'final warning'. Which we all know is teacher-speak for 'Cross me again and I'll lock you in a cupboard.' Luckily **LUCY** doesn't seem to be avoiding **JOSH** any more than usual, so it looks like the diary worked.

At break I got out the cookies and set up a stall in the playground. Before long I had a crowd of cookie-grabbing children gathered round me. I told them all to vote **FIN SPENCER** for Prom King and everybody seemed impressed. Until they bit into the cookies. Apparently the cookies had a weird broccoli aftertaste. Soon everyone was spitting them into the bin. **BRAD RADLEY** called them the most disgusting cookies ever invented and announced another new slogan for my Prom King campaign:

FIN SPENCER LEAVES A BAD TASTE IN YOUR MOUTH

Everyone laughs and soon I'm left with a table of half-eaten cookies. I guess I should have washed up the broccoli bake stuff before getting started on the cookies. Too late now, though.

I gather up the burnt broccoli biscuits

and throw them away. **JOSH** tries to cheer me up by telling me they tasted better than school dinners. Not helping, **JOSH**. I remind him of band practice tonight and head off to class.

Just as I'm waiting to go into history I catch people looking at me funny. At first I think it's because of the cookies but then **BLAKE ROMNEY** runs up and shows me a video on his phone. It's called 'Crazy Dance Boy' and it's a video of ME dancing in my bedroom last night. I have to admit, I don't look as good as I thought I did. Apparently the clip's gone viral! I can't believe my eyes. Who saw me dancing in my bedroom last night, and who would be mean enough to upload it to the internet?

ELLIE!

No wonder she was happy to give me some peace and quiet. She had a sneaky plan all along. She must have put the camera through the crack in the door and filmed me practising!

Then I realise something: this is online bullying!

I grab **BLAKE**'s phone and run straight down to the headteacher's office to show Mr Finch. He agrees that it's terrible, but there's nothing he can do because **ELLIE** doesn't go to this school. As I turn to leave I notice he's smirking and typing 'Crazy Dance Boy' into his own computer. Traitor.

I don't know what's worse, everyone seeing you dancing in your bedroom or admitting that you've just been online-bullied by your little sister. I go back to history class and as I take my seat **BRAD** leans over and winks at me.

Looking forward to seeing some of those moves on Saturday, Prom Loser

So far this week I've been made to look like a dummy with my baby pic, choked everyone on my *broccoli biscuits* and now I've gone viral dancing like a lunatic in my bedroom. And it's only Tuesday. Who's going to vote for a kid like that to be Prom King?

At lunch I sit by myself in the canteen. **JOSH** and **SAM** join me and tell me to cheer up, they'll still vote for me. It doesn't make me feel any better, though — two votes doesn't make a Prom King. But then **LUCY** comes over and sits down next to **JOSH** and I have an idea. I nudge **SAM** and he and I go and sit on another table, leaving **JOSH** and **LUCY** alone. It's time to let the romance blossom. We end up sitting next to **CLAUDIA**, but I'm too busy checking how **LUCY** and **JOSH** are getting along to pay her that much attention.

After school I tell **JOSH** and **CHARLES** that we'll rehearse after I've got my new haircut. It's costing me a fortune so it had better be good. I've never paid for my own haircut before, usually Mum's friend Patricia comes round and does it in the kitchen. I always end up looking like a choirboy. Thank goodness for spikey gel! As I make my way into KOOL KUTZ I know I've made the right choice – this place is trendy with a capital T!

I'm shown to a big chair by a guy called Gideon, given a Coke and then asked 'What do you want today?' I thought that would be obvious. I want a haircut! Duh! But it seems he's asking what type of haircut I want. Erm . . .

Gideon can see I'm struggling so he asks me what it's for. As I explain all about the prom and wanting to look good, his eyes light up.

So you want something cool and fashionable, he says.

I nod my head. Cool and fashionable are my middle names. (Well, they're actually Sebastian and Joseph, but you get the idea.) Gideon says he knows exactly what to do, which we all know is hairdresser-speak for 'I'm gonna make you look a million dollars.'

Finally, I can relax.

I must have drifted off because when I wake up Gideon's finished and I can't believe my eyes! What has this idiot done? I've got some kind of pudding bowl fringe with a ponytail. Why would he do that?

I look like that Swedish detective from Das Kop Shau.

Gideon is grinning at me like a parrot in a seed shop. 'It's called the Klaus Cut,' he says. 'It's bang on trend. Everyone wants one!'

Everyone apart from me, that is. I'm so shocked I can't say anything, which Gideon mistakes for happiness. Thanks, Gideon. You've ruined my life.

Who goes to a prom looking like a Swedish detective?

I want to go straight home and attack my own head with scissors, but then I remember band practice. I pull up my hood and scurry to school.

I'm a little bit late, but when **JOSH** and **CHARLES** see me they soon cheer up. In fact they can't stop laughing and spend the first half of the rehearsal calling me Klaus. **Ha ha.** When they break into the theme from Das Kop Shau <u>I lose it!</u> If that's how they want to be, **they don't deserve me as a lead singer.** I put down my guitar and head off in a sulk.

On my way home I stop by the shop for a cheer-me-up bag of sweets.

FIN SPENCER'S RIGHT ROYAL RULE 6
SWEETS MAKE EVERYTHING BETTER.

As I'm paying I notice there's some reduced fake tan on the counter. Fake tan. Now there's an idea! Everyone would vote for me if I looked as bronzed as a Brazilian bodybuilder! I count out some cash and buy a can.

When I get home Mum and Dad are shocked by my hair. They didn't know I liked Das Kop Shau so much. . .

I HATE Das Kop Shau! Das Kop Shau has ruined my life!

The only thing that cheers me up is the amount of trouble **ELLIE** gets into when I tell them all about the viral video, but then she says she was only getting her own back for me being so rude about her violin practice. Mum and Dad say we're 'both as bad as each other' which we all know is parent-speak for 'Ellie's wrong but we can't say so' and I promise to be kind about her violin if she takes down the video.

Before this day can get any worse, I head upstairs. My haircut might be a

but my tan is going to be radiant! When I go to use it I can see WHY it was reduced.

The label's come away so I can't read the instructions properly. Well, how hard can it be? If I leave it on overnight it should have plenty of time to work.

Fake tan applied, it's time to use the diary. I need to put things right starting with this haircut.

I never went to KOOL KUTZ, OK, diary? This haircut does not exist. While we're at it I didn't bring the cookies into school this morning, either. If I don't have to go to school as Klaus tomorrow, and I haven't given everybody the world's most disgusting cookies today then I might, just might, be in with a chance of becoming Prom King and winning CLAUDIA back.

WEDNESDAY

When I wake up I run straight to the mirror. The good news is I no longer look like a Swedish detective. The bad news is it looks like I've been **holidaying in a volcano**. The fake tan has turned my skin bright orange. I run to the bathroom and try to rub it off but it's not happening! **What am I going to do?** I can't go to school like this!

I go downstairs and **ELLIE** laughs her

155

face off! She's about to get out her phone to shoot another video when Mum stops her. Finally, some support. But when Mum scrubs at my face I can tell she's trying not to laugh too!

I notice Mum's having leftover broccoli cookies for breakfast. Thanks to the diary I didn't take them to school after all! Result! Mum thinks they're delicious — I should have known — and wants me to make her a fresh batch tonight. So I make a deal. If Mum and Dad let me stay home from school today I'll make them as many broccoli cookies as they can eat. . . .

Mum and Dad aren't having any of it. They've got an all-day hospital appointment and they don't want me staying home alone.

But then Mum has an idea. She says I can wear some of her make-up. I can't believe my ears. How is going to school in lipstick and mascara going to make me any less of a laughing stock?

Mum explains about this stuff called foundation. You smear it on your face to make you look pale. Hmmm . . . it might just work. We head upstairs, and for the first time in my life I let my mum give me a makeover. By the time she's finished my skin's actually looking pretty good. Definitely better than the time I let ELLIE do it! Sure, the inside of my nostrils are as orange as a cheesy wotsit but who's going to look up there? I might just get away with this!

I head to school and when I get to the gates **JOSH** and **CHARLIE** are waiting for me. The good news is they don't seem to notice I'm wearing make-up. Maybe Mum's idea was a good one after all!

After break we have P.E. again. Luckily, Mr Bucklestrap has decided that American Football isn't for him. Instead we spend the next half hour running around the gym jumping over obstacles. It's going well until I work up quite a sweat, which means my make-up starts to run.

JOSH is the first to notice. He says

Why's your face melting, Fin?

I try to hide it from everyone by lurking at the back and then as soon as Mr Bucklestrap blows his whistle for the end of the lesson I race into the changing rooms. I do my best to smear what's left of the make-up back into place and it's all going well until Mr Bucklestrap comes in to check we've all had our showers. I was trying to dodge mine, but Bucklestrap insists.

When I step out of the shower cubicle, everyone stops what they're doing and stares at my bright orange face. The make up is completely gone and I look like a satsuma! **BRAD** is the first to laugh and says,

Look, it's crispy-face Fin!

I want the floor to open up and swallow me whole. Mr Bucklestrap says it makes me look, 'very healthy' — apparently he uses fake tan too and wants to compare notes! **No!** I'm not chatting fake tan with a psycho P. E. teacher.

As I leave the changing rooms, I know I can do one of two things: I can either spend the rest of the day hiding, or just front it out and pretend I'm not embarrassed.

FIN SPENCER'S RIGHT ROYAL RULE 7

WHEN EVERYTHING'S GONE AS BADLY AS IT CAN POSSIBLY GO, IT'S TIME TO STOP TRYING!

I decide to front it out. I tell everyone that I'm just getting into the spirit of the prom theme. It's 'Movie Glamour', after all, so I've got myself a 'Hollywood tan'. Much to my amazement this actually works. Soon I'm getting noticed everywhere and my name is on everyone's lips – just right if you want to be named Prom King. BLAKE ROMNEY comes over and compliments me for being such a good sport.

He says:

You really are the fattest person I know

Charming. Even **CLAUDIA** comes over to have a look. She smiles and says that the fake tan makes me 'really stand out', which we all know is **CLAUDIA**-speak for, 'You're the most handsome man in school, marry me!'

The only person not happy is **BRAD RADLEY**. I can tell he's starting to worry about how much attention I'm getting when he calls me out in the lunch queue.

Oh look, he says.

It's pizza for lunch. I hope it's thin and crispy just like Fin's face!

Everyone laughs.

I've had enough of **BRAD**. It doesn't seem to matter what I do, he always takes the mickey. He's a bully and everyone knows it. Someone should do something about it, but I'm not in the mood so I keep my mouth shut and shuffle up to the counter.

I grab my pizza and try to find somewhere to sit. I spot **JOSH** and head over, but then I notice **LUCY** sitting opposite him.

They're sitting on their own, giggling and laughing.

I decide to leave them to it, gulp down my pizza and head for the computer room. My prom to-do list is getting shorter, but I still need to get a tuxedo. I search online and find a hire shop in town. That'll do! I can order it on the internet with my Paypal account and get it delivered to my house. As I'm typing in my measurements I remember what **BLAKE** said about me being his 'fat friend' and decide to get a tuxedo a couple of sizes smaller. That'll give me an incentive to work out before prom night. This Prom King is going to look like royalty.

There's a couple of minutes before the end of lunchtime so I have a look on the school bulletin board to check for any last minute prom updates. Just as I'm triple checking the start time **BRAD** sticks his head through the door.

I bought you some ORANGE juice, Fin, but it looks like you've had enough!

He heads off, laughing at his own rubbish joke.

It's the final straw. I've had enough of **BRAD RADLEY**! I click on the message board and start a new thread called '**BRAD RADLEY** is a Big Bully.' I type in all the things that annoy me about him. I say he's a bully who nobody likes and he doesn't deserve to be Prom King. I'm not going to post it, I just want to get it off my chest. It feels better to see it all written down. Just as I'm about to delete it, Mr Minchin the computer science teacher barges through the door. I jump, and instead of clicking 'delete' I click 'post'.

Nooooo!

I scrabble to undo what I've done, but Mr Minchin won't let me. It's time for lessons. He hurries me out of the door. What am I going to do? I just cross my fingers and hope no one notices.

No such luck. Fifteen minutes before the end of school Mr Finch calls me to his office. He's got the bulletin board up and he's very disappointed in me. My heart starts to thump like a rabbit with an itchy paw. I tell him I can explain, but he's not listening. He can't believe I did this so soon after our online bullying chat. I tell him it was a mistake and he agrees, it WAS. Mr Finch thinks the race to be Prom King has gone to my head, and now I'm using dirty tricks to secure votes. Dirty tricks! *I'm* not the one who put up posters of my opponent as a baby! Mr Finch explains he didn't see any evidence of that, but the evidence of what *I* have done is there for all to see.

I knew I'd get a stern telling-off, maybe a detention at worst, but Mr Finch goes one better. He tells me that he doesn't think an online bully is made of the right stuff for **Prom King** and he's taking my name off the nomination list.

I tell him he can't do that! He tells me that as headteacher he can do whatever he likes. **This is so unfair! BRAD RADLEY** is going to be **Prom King, CLAUDIA** is going to be **Prom Queen**, they're going to live happily ever after and I'm going to end up crying in a bin. **I had to do something fast.**

The school bell went and I ran straight home to fetch this diary. I needed to be back on that ballot paper. It's the most important thing ever! **So I made sure the diary was crystal clear:**

I didn't type anything online about **BRAD**

RADLEY. I didn't even pretend. It just stayed in my head, OK?

Right. With that sorted out I went downstairs to watch some TV. It's then that I see **ELLIE** playing with her badge-maker and I have an idea. Campaign badges! That's what I need! With everyone wearing Prom King **FIN** badges soon the whole school will know who to vote for!

I bribe her five pounds to show me how to use it and soon we're a little badge-making factory. By the time Mum and Dad come in to watch Das Kop Shau we've got a hundred at least. They smile. Dad says it's nice to see us getting along for a change.

Afterwards I head upstairs and search the internet for a training routine that's going to help me get in shape. I find one being done by this guy with more muscles than Arnold Schwarzenegger. We'll soon see who's **BLAKE**'s fat friend now. By the time I'm finished I'm aching all over, but it'll be worth it. With a new physique, some ace badges, and my name back in the running, Prom King is mine for the taking.

Come on, diary, I command you to make it happen. You have to listen. I'm royalty. Almost.

THURSDAY

When I woke up this morning I could barely stand up straight. I looked like some kind of weird new superhero – prawn boy! Who knew getting fit would be so painful? I limp downstairs for breakfast. Mum asks why I'm walking like a sprained spider and I explain about trying to get in shape for the prom. ELLIE laughs and says the only shape I got into was a triangle. Ha! Ha! Ha! NOT.

I would say something mean back, but then I remember she did help me out with the badges last night so I guess she's not all bad.

After washing up the breakfast things and tidying the lounge I make my way to school. **The good news** is I'm back on the nomination list. Nobody seems to know anything about the stuff I posted on the internet. **The bad news** is **BRAD** is being as annoying as ever. He's just jealous — I'm on track to be **Prom King** and he isn't. My new badges are going to seal the deal!

JOSH and I spend first break handing out badges and taking down names. If someone says they'll vote for me for **Prom King,**

they get a badge. By the end of break time we've spoken to almost everyone in our year group and it's close. Lee and Patrick in the other classes seem pretty popular and <u>the bad news</u> is it looks like everyone is planning on voting for the Prom King candidate from their class. <u>The good news</u> is my class has more people in it than the others. If I can get them ALL to vote for me then I'll be Prom King, but with **BRAD** running as well that might be tough.

As I'm heading back in for class Mr Burchester stops me. He's written a song for the prom and he wants everybody who is performing to play it together at the end of the night. No way! System of the Future are a rock band.

We don't play with music teachers. Mr Burchester explains that Mr Finch has said if we don't play his song then we won't be playing at all. It's not fair! But I agree to give up my lunch break so we can all rehearse. I tell **CHARLES** and **JOSH** about it before class.

The next lesson is art and **BLAKE** has persuaded Mrs Skiffington the art teacher to let us make some decorations for the prom. Some people are painting banners, others are making streamers. I get stuck making centrepieces. I don't even know what a centrepiece is. It turns out they're decorations that you stick in the centre of tables. The ones for the prom are going to be lame little statues covered in flowers.

I'm basically spending my art lesson flower arranging. **Not cool!**

I don't really listen to the instructions. I mean how hard can it be to decorate a statue? **Really hard**, it turns out. I didn't realise how sticky the glue was and before long I've got a load of flowers and a statue stuck to my hand. It's a

JOSH comes over and tries to help me pull them off before anyone notices, but it feels like he's trying to skin me alive and I end up screaming like **an opera singer who's just stubbed his toe!** Mrs Skiffington sees what's happened and sends me down to

the nurse. I spend the next two hours sitting with my hand in a bowl of warm soapy water waiting for the flowers to soak off.

By the time the nurse lets me go I've missed most of lunch. Luckily that means I've also missed most of Mr Burchester's prom band rehearsal. **CHARLES** and **JOSH** haven't, however, and when I arrive they look like they're about to kill me.

When I hear the terrible song I begin to realise why. The lyrics are awful and the tune sounds like someone strangling an octopus.

**It's time to celebrate
The end of year
End of year
End of year.**

**It's time to celebrate
Prom is here
Prom is here
Hooray!**

I try my best to join in, but my hands are still a little bit sticky from all the flower glue so my guitar sounds terrible. In a way I think it improves the song. To be honest, a chainsaw would improve that song!

As I'm heading back to class I run into **BLAKE ROMNEY**. He reminds me that I agreed to organise a prom photographer.

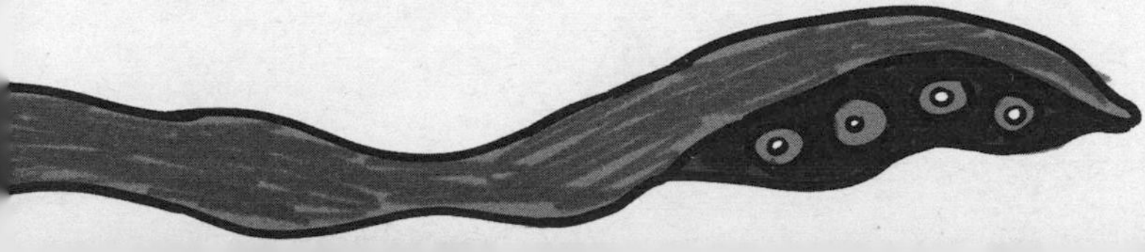

This is the first I've heard of it! He says I agreed to the whole thing at the very first meeting. I don't remember that, but then I had been very excited at the thought of playing with the band so I might have done.

I confess that I haven't booked anyone yet, but he says he's sure he can rely on his 'fat friend'. **What is wrong with this guy?** I decide to tell him to his face that in this country what he is saying is very rude. **BLAKE** gets upset and says he didn't mean to offend anyone. I tell him that he has offended me – **big time** – and that if he can't understand why then he may as well head back to America.

BLAKE gets angry then and says that if that's the way I feel then I can't have a lift

178

in his limo to the prom, and storms off.

<u>That's all I need!</u> Now I've got two more jobs to add to my list:

Get my own limo to the prom
Find a photographer

Just before lessons **JOSH** runs up. He's written a song for **LUCY** and wants to practise it tonight. He starts to sing me a bit.

'Lucy!
Your eyes are like the blue sea
You make me want to boogie
And make my heart go gooey
— Lucy!

Lucy!
You're my favourite cutie
I love you more than sushi
Lucy!'

BARF!

I'm about to tell him, **STOP!** It's terrible! when I realise girls like that kind of thing and it might just get me **CLAUDIA** back as a date. So instead I tell him he should sing it to her and ask her for a date to the prom – then, when she says yes, I'll step in and offer to take **CLAUDIA**. What could possibly go wrong?

The rest of the day flies past and when I get home there's a package waiting for me. It's the tuxedo from the shop. I try it on, but it doesn't fit. I suck in my tummy and hold my breath but it's no use. This tuxedo is smaller than a microbe's mini skirt.

That's something else to add to my list of worries.

I'm about to take it back to the shop when Dad stops me. He's on his way to a Swedish furniture barn and he wants me to come and help. What is it with my parents and Sweden? I'm thinking of changing my name to Sven. Besides I haven't time for this. **I've got my own stuff to sort out!** But he points to the fridge list of doom. **Apparently I agreed!** He offers to drop me off at the tuxedo shop on the way home. It's as good as it's going to get so I agree to go.

We're shopping for things for the baby. We need a new cot and a chest of drawers. Shopping for *babies* is rubbish. The only thing that makes it bearable is when

Dad buys us dinner in the café and I break my own record for eating meatballs. **Thirteen in one minute!**

We cram all the boxes into the car but when Dad turns the key the engine won't start. **Not again!** Dad calls the AA and they take two hours to arrive. They get the car going, but it's wheezing like an elephant on an exercise bike. By the time we drive past the tuxedo shop it's closed. Dad says that I shouldn't worry, he's got a tuxedo in the loft I can borrow.

It sounds like I *should* worry, but I don't have time to because when I get home Dad makes me help him put together all the flat-pack furniture we've just bought. This is a

I don't know the first thing about putting together a cot! As it turns out, neither does Dad, and it's nearly midnight by the time we finish. I am so excited about hammering in the final nail that I miss and hit my thumb. I scream so loud the bedroom windows shake.

Before I go to bed I have a quick look online to see if I can book myself a limo, but the local place says it's SOLD OUT! Surely they'll still have something? I'll call in tomorrow. As I'm setting my alarm I see JOSH has phoned me fifteen times too. Maybe he wants to sing me the next sixteen verses of his terrible song for LUCY? Thankfully it's too late to call now, I'll catch up with him tomorrow.

By the time I finally get to bed my thumb is really swollen. **Uh oh.** With my thumb this big there's no way I'm going to be able to play guitar on Saturday. **I need the diary to fix it.** What else needs fixing from today? It would be good to get back in **BLAKE**'s good books, so that I still have a ride to the prom, but he **DOES** keep calling me fat. If he thinks that about me then maybe I don't want to be in his limo.

I decide to leave things the way they are and find my own transportation. It would be good to get a bigger tuxedo, but then I remember I ordered it yesterday, so it's too late to do that. I'll just have to do my best to fix it all in the morning. That's if the diary can make sure I didn't hit my thumb with a hammer.

OK, diary? Instead of bashing myself I was extra careful and missed by miles. I can't have a mutant thumb for prom! Royalty do a lot of waving and that would just look weird.

FRIDAY

You thought yesterday was bad? Well, today was a

Right now I should be kicking back and getting ready to be crowned **Prom King** tomorrow night. Instead, I'm kicking myself that so much has gone wrong. **Where to begin?**

The day started out fine enough. My thumb was back to its normal size so I was ready to rock out with **System of the Future.** But before I could get to school I had my **chore list** to plough through.

By the time I got to school I was already in a bad mood. **CHARLES** and **JOSH** were waiting for me at the school gates and they **didn't look pleased. JOSH** asked if I'd got his messages. I hadn't even checked my phone this morning! I told them I was a busy person, I couldn't be expected to reply to messages.

CHARLES huffed and said, 'You can't be expected to come to band rehearsals either.' My blood ran cold. **Of course!** Last night's band rehearsal. **I'd completely forgotten.**

I promised to be at the next one but **CHARLES** said that didn't matter.

I was fired.

For a moment I thought my ears were broken. How could I be fired from my own band? I turned to **JOSH**. This was some sort of joke, right? Apparently it wasn't. When I didn't turn up last night they had a vote and kicked me out. **CHARLES** was going to be lead singer at the prom.

JOSH said he didn't want to look silly in front of his new girlfriend **LUCY**, so System of the Future was now a duo. Before I had chance to say anything the bell rang and **CHARLES** and **JOSH** headed off to lessons.

This could not be happening to me.

System of the Future was MY

band. All of my plans were falling down around my ears. It was a

I **HAD** to play at the prom. When people heard how good I was they'd all vote for me as Prom King, **I was sure of it.** I needed to figure something out.

At break I went to find **CLAUDIA**. I might not have a band to play in but at least I had a chance at a date, right? WRONG! Lucy **was** going with **JOSH**, but that didn't mean **CLAUDIA** wanted to go with me. She'd decided to go with nobody. That was just <u>brilliant</u>. I was being dumped for nobody.

I tried to plead with **CLAUDIA**. She *had* to change her mind. To try and make her feel sorry for me I explained about all the terrible things that had been happening to me. I explained about being kicked out of my own band, about **BLAKE ROMNEY** kicking me out of his limo, about my too-small tuxedo, my bright orange face . . . everything!

CLAUDIA didn't bat an eyelid. She said that I seemed to be spending a great deal of time thinking about myself, and not about anyone else. This prom was supposed to be for everybody, not just for me. Maybe I should remember that. Ouch.

Before she left she reminded me about the prom photographer. She hoped it was all in hand. My heart began to thud.

The photographer! I'd have to work something out this evening.

I spend the rest of the day trying to salvage the one thing that might actually make this whole prom thing worthwhile — being voted Prom King. **BRAD RADLEY** is pulling out all the stops too. He's brought in a bumper box of chocolate bars and was handing them out left, right and centre. How am I supposed to compete with that?

By home time all anyone is talking about is the prom tomorrow. Everyone seems really excited about it and they're not even up for Prom King. They just seem to be looking forward to a fun party. Perhaps **CLAUDIA** is right. If I'd spent the last two weeks looking forward to celebrating with my friends rather than trying to get myself elected to royalty, then I might have enjoyed this whole prom thing more. I wish I hadn't put myself down for Prom King at all.

Unfortunately my magic diary doesn't work that far back.

On the way home I called in at the limo shop to see what they could lend me so I could arrive in style. Outside there were loads of really cool limos and a Lamborghini and a couple of Porsches too. This was the place for me! I marched up to the counter and asked the spotty guy behind the desk if they had something for me.

He laughed and pointed to a rusty old bike chained to the railings. Ha! Ha! Ha! Very funny!

NOT. Didn't he know he was dealing with almost-royalty?

Turns out it didn't matter as everything they had was already reserved.

I begged the guy. They must have something.

He laughed and pointed to the rusty old bike again.

It wasn't any funnier the second time.

Just as I was about to leave he stopped me. They did have one thing available, but it was very expensive and they only used it on special occasions.

Very expensive means very good, right? And what occasion could be more special than a prom? It was going to clear out the rest of my cash, but I paid the guy and gave him my address. He said the driver would be there by six tomorrow.

Result! Who needs **BLAKE** and his snazzy limo?

When I get home Dad is smiling at me and I get worried. What new horrible chore has he dreamed up for me NOW?

1 Alphabetising the freezer drawers?

2 Cleaning the loo brush?

3 Counting his eyebrow hairs?

But it turns out he's just fished out his old tuxedo from the attic. The good news is it fits. <u>**The bad news**</u> is that it's bright blue, smells of cat wee and has flares!

Flares through the ages

It's more a tuxe-DON'T than a tuxe-DO!

I can't wear that! But what choice do I have? I can't go naked!

I leave Mum and Dad watching Das Kop Shau and discussing baby names. Apparently if he's a boy he's going to be Johan, after the bad guy in the show. Poor kid. Stay in there for as long as you can! Things only get tougher the older you get.

I head upstairs and try to figure out what I'm going to do. **I've got no band, no date, I'm still bright orange and my tuxedo is a relic from a time before the dinosaurs.** Just when I think things can't get any worse, **ELLIE** cranks up her violin. I'm about to scream at her to stop when I realise she's playing an **X-WING** song. **Maybe she is getting better . . .** In fact, it sounds **pretty good**. I still wish she'd stop, though.

I remember why I stopped using this diary now — it doesn't always make things better. **Sometimes it makes things worse!** If I want to fix my prom then I'll have to fix it on my own — but how? It's too late now, **the damage is done.**

Perhaps you get the prom you deserve. I've been trying to magic my way to success instead of just doing the right thing. It's time to stop.

Diary, today I change . . .

. . . nothing!

My prom is going to be a

area. That's all right. I'm a

area too!

SATURDAY

You'll never guess where I'm writing this diary from, and quite frankly I never expected to end up here tonight. But we'll get to that. **Let's start at the beginning.**

I actually woke up feeling OK about things this morning. I was so certain that my prom couldn't get any worse I'd decided to get on and enjoy it by being myself. Sure I had no date, no band and there was **no way** I was going to be Prom King, but nothing else could go wrong, right?

WRONG.

When I woke up there was a text from **BLAKE ROMNEY** reminding me that I'd better have a photographer lined up for tonight or the whole thing would be ruined. My heart sank. I'd been so busy, I'd completely forgotten again. There was no way I was going to find anyone now, but I couldn't tell **BLAKE** that, he was already angry with me. I just texted back:

No Problemo.

Predictive text decided to change it to:

Go Pablo.

Thanks, phone. You're not helping!

BLAKE sent back a confused message asking why we were having a Mexican photographer? I decided just to quit while I was ahead.

When I got downstairs Dad was fiddling with his camera. Apparently he's almost got the knack now. Wait . . . I need a photographer, Dad has a camera and he can **almost, nearly** use it. What was the worst that could happen?

Sure, it meant going to the prom with my dad — not the coolest thing I've ever done in my life — but at least I wouldn't be letting everyone down. I knew all my friends would be dressed up and hoping for photos to remember their first (and only) prom. Besides, when you've resigned yourself to being a loser, what does it matter?

Dad was actually pretty pleased to be invited along as prom photographer. He went straight to the tuxedo shop to hire an outfit. I thought about going with him, but I'd blown the last of my cash at the limo shop. Typical — I would be turning up in some disco monstrosity and he was going to look the bee's knees!

I started getting dressed at four o'clock so that I would be ready for when my hot ride turned up. I had a shower, did my hair, didn't like how I'd done my hair and had another shower, did my hair again and then sprayed myself with some of Dad's aftershave. By the time I finally squeezed myself into the bright blue tuxedo I was looking as good as I could – if a little orange.

I went downstairs to wait. Mum was sitting on the sofa watching TV, and Dad was checking his camera was charged. He was wearing a tuxedo too, a black one. Just before six Mum started to feel poorly and headed upstairs for a lie-down. Dad got worried and wanted to stay and I started to panic. Luckily Mum said it was 'Nothing', which we all know is mum-speak for 'Something, but I'm going to make you guess what it is.' Dad still didn't want to go to the prom because Mum needed to rest, and there was no one to look after **ELLIE**.

I was desperate. I needed Dad to be there. If that meant **ELLIE** had to come with us too then so be it . . .

So I did have a date for the prom after all. My six-year-old kid sister. Kill me now!

Just then there was a loud honk and the sound of an engine revving outside. The limo had arrived! Sort of.

It turns out that the limo guy's idea of 'something special' was a bright red double-decker bus. ELLIE was over the moon. I wanted my money back. The driver explained it was something they only hired out for special occasions, usually weddings. It was take the bus or walk. It looked like I had no choice.

Dad and ELLIE piled on and I took a seat up top, as far from them as possible. As we drove off ELLIE rang the bell every five seconds. Way to go, sis! Like we need to attract any more attention.

No sooner had we got out of the drive than we were caught up in a traffic jam, and as we trundled towards the lights I could see why. Two limos had crashed into each other and as we got closer I could see that **BLAKE**, **JOSH**, **SAM** and **CHARLES** were standing beside one and **BRAD RADLEY** and his gang were standing beside the other.

Nobody was hurt, but the two limo drivers were arguing and it didn't look like anyone would be going anywhere fast.

As we drove past I wanted to duck so no one would see me in a stupid bus. But then I had another idea. I ran downstairs and told the bus driver to pull over, then I poked my head out of the window.

'Need a lift?' I asked.

BLAKE grinned and so did **BRAD** and soon we were all piled onto the bus and heading to the prom together. **BLAKE** and I sat right at the back up top. He said that this was the nicest thing anyone could have done. He knew I was fat.

What was he playing at? I'd just given him a lift to prom on my bus and he was still calling me fat! I decided to have it out with him there and then:

I am not fat!

Blake laughed and said that he wasn't calling me fat as in **eaten-too-many-burgers fat**. He was calling me *phat* as in <u>**cooler than cool**</u>. It wasn't even spelled the same way. **Typical!** How was I to know that 'phat' was **American for ace?**

Phat rapper   Fat rapper

All this time I'd thought he had **been insulting me** when actually he'd been paying me **a massive compliment**.

As we drove to school, we started to pass more and more of our friends walking to the prom. Every time we did we slowed down so they could pile onto the bus. **JOSH** and **LUCY** took the front seat and **CLAUDIA** sat on the back seat with me and **BLAKE**. She looked amazing and she smiled when she saw my blue flares! Amazingly, they matched the flowers she was wearing in her hair! Soon we had **a whole party bus full of people**. I asked the driver to turn on the radio and **X-WING** started to blast out.

For the first time since this whole prom thing started, I was actually enjoying myself!

We pulled into school and everyone hopped off. If I'd wanted people to notice me, they noticed me! There's nothing like pulling up to the prom in your own double-decker bus with your dad, your kid sister and all your mates on board. The party had arrived!

As we headed into the school hall everyone complimented me on my tuxedo. All the other boys had gone for something black and boring. I was the only one who had been 'individual' enough to do something different. Of course it was all a mistake, but they didn't need to know that, did they?

Before System of the Future started to play, JOSH went to speak to CHARLES to see if he'd let me back in the band. **CHARLES** said it wasn't about whether I was in the band or not, he just didn't want to play with someone he hadn't rehearsed with. To be honest, I got that, and rather than make a scene I told **JOSH** it was OK. They got up and started to play and soon everyone was dancing — including me!

This was great. Up on the stage, singing with the band, I wouldn't have been able to actually enjoy the prom. But out on the dancefloor, with my school friends, I was part of the gang and it was brilliant. I busted out some of the moves I'd learned from the internet and soon everyone was joining in. If the viral video of me dancing had done one thing, it had made sure everyone knew the same routine! **BLAKE** came and danced next to me and soon we were synchronising. **BLAKE** called it doing 'The Phat Fin', which sounded good to me.

After Mr Burchester's band On the Fiddle had played, which **ELLIE** loved a bit too much if you ask me, **SAM LUTHER** asked when he was going to sing his song with me. I explained that it couldn't happen as I didn't have a band any more. **SAM** said that didn't matter, he wanted to sing with me not the band. That was nice of him but what were we going to sing? Then I had a brainwave. **ELLIE** was getting really good at the violin, she even knew one of my favourite **X-WING** songs. I knew it would mean a lot to her to play it in front of all these people. So I borrowed one of Mr Burchester's fiddles and

asked her to join us. **ELLIE** wasn't too sure
— she'd only ever practised in her bedroom.
I promised her it would be fine. **CHARLES**
lent me his guitar and we took to the stage.

When **SAM** opened his mouth to sing, the
most amazing voice came out. It was like a
TV talent show moment. This guy sang
like an angel. Everyone stood and listened.

It was an even better acoustic reworking of the original! When we had finished, everyone clapped and cheered. Mr Burchester came over and offered **ELLIE** a starring role in On the Fiddle. She gave me a massive hug. Sometimes being a big brother is cool.

Then **BLAKE** announced it was time for the vote. Everyone wrote the names of the Prom King and Queen they wanted on the back of their tickets and popped them in the ballot box. I voted for **BRAD** because I didn't want to be the only one voting for myself — how desperate would that look?

When all the votes had been counted **BLAKE** stood on stage and read out the results.

'This year's Prom Queen is . . .
CLAUDIA RONSON!'

Well, that was obvious, but who was she going to be dancing with?

'And the Prom King,' continued BLAKE, 'is . . .

FIN SPENCER!'

I couldn't believe my ears. Perhaps BLAKE couldn't count. All eyes were on me and everyone was clapping. The band struck up a song, CLAUDIA and I were given a crown each, and soon we were dancing.

CLAUDIA could see I was shocked. I told her I didn't think anyone would vote for me. She smiled and said, 'Who wouldn't vote for you?' Well, I explained, I was wearing a bright blue tuxedo, I'd arrived in a bus with my dad and my little sister and I'd been banned from my own band.

CLAUDIA laughed. 'Or, to put it another way, you saved the day with the bus, danced your socks off, found a great photographer, got your sister to play at the prom and discovered a guy with a great voice. You finally stopped making this prom about you and made it about everyone else instead.'

I finally got it. So I apologised to her for not letting her audition for the band and hoped she forgave me. She smiled and said she'd get a chance to show me her guitar skills one day!

And as I danced with **CLAUDIA** with a crown on my head I couldn't believe my luck.

Before we knew it, the prom was over way too soon and we all piled back on the bus. After we'd dropped everyone home the bus took **ELLIE**, Dad and me back to our house.

When we got in, Mum was in a panic. The baby was coming!

Dad rushed outside and tried to get the car started.

It wouldn't start. It sounded like a grizzly bear with a chest cold. The bus was just disappearing round the corner.

I had to stop it!

I ran after it, waving my arms until the driver noticed me.

We jumped on — well, Mum hobbled — and the driver raced to the hospital as fast as he could. Which is pretty fast! That's where I am now. In a hospital waiting room, with a crown on my head.

So, diary, there's nothing to change tonight.

I'm Prom King and I did it all without you — kind of! Now, if you'll excuse me I need to go. It's time to meet my new baby brother or sister.

SUNDAY

This morning I am still **Prom King** AND I have a new little sister! We have no idea what she's called yet. Mum and Dad were so certain the baby was going to be a boy they didn't even bother thinking of any girls' names. I think Finella has a nice ring to it, but we shall see!

Our race to the hospital got on the news. They sent round a photographer and this morning we're front page of the local paper.

There's a big picture of all of us by the big red bus with the headline 'Express Delivery.' **My little sister's already famous!** Not bad for a baby that doesn't even have a name yet. She's following in my footsteps!

Who knows, she may even grow up to be a **Prom Queen** herself one day. If she's interested in finding out how to do it, I can even give her the recipe for broccoli cookies.

When we got home, **CLAUDIA** and **JOSH** came round to see the new baby. Apparently **CHARLES** wants to give me my place in the band back, providing I turn up for rehearsals this time. I'm about to agree, but then **I have a thought**. This **prom** has unlocked so much hidden talent. There's **CLAUDIA** on guitar, **SAM** the singer, **ELLIE** on the violin and when **CLIFF** gets back from America we'll need to fit him in somewhere too. I think it's time to put **System of the Future** to bed and break out **a new band,** one that's big enough for all of us. I even know what to call it – **The Kings and Queens of Rock!**

JOSH and **CLAUDIA** think it's a great idea and I'm sure everyone else will too. From the wailing noises my new little sister is making we may have to find space for her as a *backing singer* too!

In the afternoon **BLAKE ROMNEY** comes to say goodbye. He's heading back to America next week. I'd been so caught up in the prom I'd forgotten he was actually leaving. I apologise for the 'phat' understanding and thank him for bringing the prom to our school. We hug and I tell him he'll always have a **Phat Friend** in England! He invites me over to visit him one day. Definitely, providing I can bring the rest of the band. This is turning into a perfect day! The band is only a few hours old and already we've got a tour of America in the bag!

Before he leaves he gives me his copy of **DEATH SQUADRON: ANNIHILATION** and I know he's the greatest guy that ever lived. After me, of course!

So everything is back to the way it should be, only now it's even better! I think it's time to put this diary away again. I don't need it and I'm going to be far too busy with my royal duties to write in it every day' going to be spending time rocking with my new band, and when I'm not doing that I'm going to be rocking my little sister to sleep.

222